W9-AHR-483

Lynch's Revenge

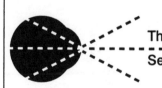

This Large Print Book carries the
Seal of Approval of N.A.V.H.

Lynch's Revenge

Jack Cummings

Thorndike Press • Thorndike, Maine

Copyright © 1985 by Jack Cummings

All rights reserved.

Published in 1994 by arrangement with Walker Publishing Company, Inc.

All the characters and events portrayed in this story are fictitious.

Thorndike Large Print ® Western Series.

The tree indicium is a trademark of Thorndike Press.

The text of this Large Print edition is unabridged.
Other aspects of the book may vary from the original edition.

Set in 16 pt. News Plantin.

Printed in the United States on acid-free, high opacity paper. ∞

Library of Congress Cataloging in Publication Data

Cummings, Jack, 1925–
    Lynch's revenge / Jack Cummings.
      p. cm.
    ISBN 0-7862-0219-X (alk. paper : lg. print)
    1. Large type books. I. Title.
  [PS3553.U444L9 1994]
  813′.54—dc20

                                                 94-9244

For Florence, my wife

Chapter 1

The six-man patrol of Company C, Frontier Battalion of Texas Rangers, had seen the smoke rising from the ranch for an hour before they reached it.

John Kelso, the sergeant in command, was the first to ride up to the smoldering remains of the crude buildings. The ranger riding behind him said, "Comanche or Kiowa?"

Kelso shook his head, not answering as he studied the blackened desolation. He felt cold, colder than he should have under his range clothes and heavy jacket, even in that season of November 1878, there in the Texas Panhandle. At that moment he felt every one of his thirty years in every muscle of his trail-toughened body. He was a medium-tall man, without fat, and with weathered features that still looked young.

Another ranger said, "Kelso, you know the name here?"

Kelso nodded. "This was Lynch's place.

Shows on my map that way. Name of Sam Lynch."

"Looks like he was raising horses."

"Comanche bait, for sure," Kelso said. "A man raising horses out here is asking for trouble. Even at this late date."

"A man raising anything out here is asking for trouble."

"I don't see any bodies," Kelso said. "Spread out and look around."

They fanned out, riding slowly through the debris.

Kelso found Sam Lynch's body next to the harness lean-to where he'd been working when the raiders struck. There was a Comanche war arrow sticking out of his chest, and his scalp had been taken, leaving a bloody patch of his bare skull exposed.

It wasn't a neat job of scalping, as a Comanche who was in practice should have done. There had been no clean circling incision with a scalp knife. This looked like it had been crudely taken off with a dull-edged tomahawk. Not only was the scalp lock missing, the whole top of Lynch's head had been butchered. It was enough to turn Kelso's stomach.

"Leastwise they didn't torture the rest of him like they used to do," somebody said.

"Can't torture a dead man," Kelso said.

"They can hack one up something terrible,

out of pure meanness."

"Didn't take the time," Kelso said. He pointed beyond the smoking plank buildings to the empty pole corral and the open fenced pasture beyond. "Too busy taking the horses. That's what they come raiding for."

A ranger said, "Right off the Cache Creek reservation. And the murdering bastards are probably on their way back there right now."

Kelso started to say something, then stopped. He dismounted and stomped over to Sam Lynch's body and hunkered down beside it.

He stared, unbelieving. Then he said, "He's still alive. Hell, no man is that tough."

They found a light wagon which hadn't burned, and outside the pasture they spotted a team ignored by the raiding Comanches who were interested only in riding horses.

They lined the wagon bed with several blankets and picked up Sam Lynch and laid him carefully in it. Kelso said, "We got to get him to a doctor."

"You think he can live through a ride in that wagon?"

"He might. He lived through that scalping, didn't he?"

One of the rangers said, "Might be we ouht to try to pull that arrow out of him."

Kelso shook his head. "I don't want to risk it now. That arrow is damn near through him and it's barbed. And it's plugging some of the blood leak."

"Lot of miles maybe before we can find a doc."

Kelso shrugged. "Don't know of one this side of Jacksboro headquarters. That'll be our own medico, Doc Nichols."

"You're talking about a hundred-twenty-mile ride."

"Got any better ideas?"

"What about that little town we come through on the way out? Place called Bonner. Wasn't more than twenty miles back. Reckon they got a doc there?"

"We'll find out," Kelso said.

Bonner was a new town. A lot of the boards it was built with hadn't even weathered much yet. Kelso remembered that it was only three and a half years since Quanah had given up and brought the last of the Kwahadi Comanches to the reservation, and that this had been part of their stomping grounds and there had been no towns or even settlers in this part of Texas before then.

Now there was a mercantile, a saloon, a restaurant, a single-story false-front hotel, a barber shop and a few shack residences which

10

probably belonged to the business owners.

Kelso halted the detachment in front of the mercantile. He got down, let his reins drop and walked into the place.

A man of about forty, so thin he looked taller than he was, stood in front of a counter made partly from shipping boxes. He wore a white grocer's apron and black sleeve protectors. He said, "Hello, ranger. Name is Murdock. I saw you riding through yesterday. Now, already, I see you riding back."

"Got a wounded man with me," Kelso said. "You got a doctor in this town?"

"We got Rademacher."

"He's a doctor?"

"He's the barber."

"A barber?"

"Only thing we got," Murdock said. "Might be, if I take a look I can tell if he can do you any good."

"Out there in the wagon," Kelso said.

Murdock went out and over to the side of the wagon and looked at the bloody, unmoving figure on the blankets. "Hell," he said, "that's Sam Lynch. Done his trading here." He paused. "But it looks like you need a undertaker instead of a doc. But that's all right — Rademacher is one of them, too."

"He ain't dead," Kelso said.

"You sure?" Murdock bent closer to look.

11

"Yeah. It don't seem possible, but I can scc that arrow move when he breathes." He gave a strained, nervous chuckle. "One thing sure, he don't need Rademacher as a barber."

Kelso gave him a disgusted look. He said, "Get Rademacher."

"Sure." The storekeeper went down a couple of doors and entered the barber shop. Pretty soon he came out followed by a short, chunky man with graying hair and a wispy mustache, wearing a soiled smock.

The barber came over and stood fingering his mustache while he stared into the wagon.

Kelso said, "Well?"

"He don't have a chance," Rademacher said. "He ought to be dead right now."

Kelso reached out and grabbed him by the front of his smock. "You can't help him?" he said.

"I never pulled an arrow out."

Kelso kept holding the fistful of his smock.

"I know something about gunshot wounds," the barber said. "Arrows, I don't. Hell, there ain't been a Comanche raid all the time I been here, makes two years nearly."

Kelso let go of him. "You got to do something."

"Wait a little and I can bury him."

"You can't just let him die without trying —"

"If it was a gun wound, then I could maybe —"

"That arrow has got a barbed head," Kelso said. "How could I get it out?"

"It's almost through him. I guess you'd have to push it the rest of the way and then cut the head off so you could pull the shaft back out."

"You got a place where I can work on him?"

"You going to try it yourself?"

"Somebody's got to."

"Well, I got a table in back of my place I use for gunshot wounds and broken legs and such. Ought to work out for arrow pulling, I guess," Rademacher said. "I got a bag of instruments, too. I took them from a real doctor come through a few months back and died of drinking rotgut likker in Emory's saloon the first week he was here." He stopped and gave Kelso a quick look, as if he'd suddenly realized Kelso might accuse him of stealing. He said, "I buried him for free, so I figured he owed me his hand tools."

"Let's see that operating table," Kelso said.

Murdock and a couple of others followed them in. Outside the shop a crowd was beginning to gather. One of them called to Murdock, "Anybody tell Annie about this yet?"

Murdock said, "Reckon not, else she'd be

13

here. Somebody better go fetch her."

"I'll go."

The table looked all right to Kelso, and he led the way back out to the wagon to get Lynch. Once he got there, he hesitated, trying to make up his mind to do it.

Murdock said, "I guess he made a bad mistake, settling in the Panhandle. But I talked to him a couple of times and he said this was the only place left in Texas where a flat-busted ranch hand could start on his own nowadays. And he figured Colonel Mackenzie and his Fourth Cavalry had finally made believers out of them Comanches when Quanah Parker brought them in, three years back."

"So did we all," Kelso said.

Murdock shook his head. "We should have knowed better. These few years of peace got us believing what we wanted to believe. We should've knowed that, sooner or later, some hot-headed young buck was bound to jump the traces. It's in their blood. Some young buck who wants to be knowed as the last Comanche war chief."

"We know better now," Kelso said, looking at Lynch.

"The odd thing is," Murdock said, "that the first one hit had to be Lynch here. He mentioned to me once that he'd been taken captive by them Kwahadies when he was a

14

youngster, and he finally managed to get away. And now he got hit by the lightning a second time. I call that downright bad luck."

Kelso stood there, silent, thinking about this. He said, "He ever give you the particulars of his capture or his escape?"

"He didn't seem to want to talk about it much. Said he had put it all out of his mind so he could get on with everyday living. What little I gathered, his folks had been killed and their ranch burned out down San Saba way when he was twelve years old. He was took captive and used by the Comanches as a slave — tending their horse herds. That's where he learned about horses, I guess. Then, after four or five years, he sneaked off one night with a mount and a couple of spares he'd staked out in secret. He went back to San Saba and worked as a wrangler until he got it into his head to go horse raising on his own. Said he'd always remembered that spot he picked to settle on because it was different than most of this country hereabouts. You seen his place, I reckon. According to him he had good grazing out there, water nearby. The spot was more like the buffalo grass country on top the Staked Plains."

Kelso nodded. "Looked like fair horse country. Except I wouldn't pick it for raising horses. Not with them Comanch bastards starting to act up."

"He didn't know they was going to do that," Murdock said. "Neither did we. Hell, you think me and the rest of these recent settlers would have come if we guessed that?"

"I guess not."

Somebody said, "Here comes Annie," and the crowd parted a little so she could come through.

She was a pretty girl, well formed, with light-brown hair and hazel eyes. Kelso thought she was in her late twenties, but she might have been a few years younger than that. He could tell she had been around some, even though she had a naturally fine complexion without rouge or mascara, although she had colored her lips with carmine.

She pushed through to the wagon and stood looking down at Lynch, and then she gave a little cry and leaned over and looked into his face and touched his cheek. She said, "Sam. Oh, Sam!"

He had been unconscious, but just then his eyes opened and he seemed to recognize her, and Kelso thought he smiled faintly but he wasn't sure. Then his eyes closed and he was out again.

The girl straightened and there were tears in her eyes. She said, "His head — it's so awful

— they told me he'd been scalped, but —"

Kelso said nothing.

"Oh, God!" she said. "And he was so hand-some."

Her words startled Kelso. It seemed to him that was a hell of a thing to think of at a time like this. The comment angered him so that he wanted to jar her. He said in a hard voice, "He may not live." And then he wondered at his saying it, after taking offense when the townsmen had suggested the same thing. It was just that her reaction got under his skin.

He said, "You his girl?"

She hesitated, then said, "No. But he acted like it sometimes."

Rademacher spoke up. "Hell, Annie, tell him the truth. Sam wanted you to marry him and move out there on his ranch."

Kelso looked at her again. He'd heard of saloon girls doing that now and then. And some of them had turned out to be pretty good wives, although he found that hard to believe.

She said, "Poor Sam. Nothing ever worked out for him."

She turned to meet Kelso's eyes, and he saw a sad sympathy there, enough for him to make his decision. "Carry him in to that operating table," he said.

He took notice then when she slipped into the barber shop behind them. Strong, he thought. A lot of woman there.

It didn't take much pressure to push the arrow the rest of the way through Lynch. The point was just inside the skin of his back, and the arrowhead was turned so it slipped through the space between a couple of his ribs.

He groaned when Kelso gave the shaft a shove, then passed out again. Kelso cut the arrowhead off and, with two of them holding him down tight against the oil-clothed table top, got hold of the feathered end and pulled the shaft out.

A spurt of blood came with it, but the barber was standing ready with a towel and he pressed it hard against the wound, front and back, and held it there.

"That's the worst of it," the barber said. There was sweat running down his fat cheeks. "If we can get the bleeding stopped, and if he ain't got a punctured lung or something else, and if he don't get infected or fever or pneumonia or die from just hurting, he might live. That's if you can get him to a real doc in time."

"He's going to live," Kelso said. "I've made my mind up to it. What about his head?"

"You want me to give him a haircut?"

Kelso reached out and grabbed his smock front again. "That's twice I heard that joke since I been here and I'm sick of it. I ought to take one of your razors and lift *your* scalp."

Rademacher's ruddy face turned pale. He said, "I don't rightly know why I said that. It just popped out. Maybe I can fix him up a compress with hair grease on it. That might help some." He paused. "I never tended a *scalped* head before. Like I said, there ain't been no Injun raids since I been here and —"

"Fix the compress."

"Sure."

Rademacher folded up a towel and smeared a lot of hairgroom grease on it and tied it in place and they carried Lynch out and laid him in the wagon again.

All this time the girl hadn't said a word while she watched them.

Murdock said, "We all liked Sam around here, all of us that knowed him. If you ever get out this way again, stop and let us know if he made it." Then he added, "That's if any of us are still here. If those red bastards are going to start raiding some more, I'm ready to pull up stakes and leave."

Kelso said, "The tracks they left around Lynch's place showed only about a dozen of them. They ain't likely to attack a town."

"They don't need to," Murdock said. "They get to wiping out lone settlers and their families, the town will die, too."

"Let's hope this ain't the beginning of something then."

"Amen to that," Murdock said gloomily.

Kelso drew the girl off to one side and said, "So you were going to marry him and become a rancher's wife."

At first she didn't answer. Then she said, "He wanted it that way. I didn't. But he was — is — a stubborn man. He gets an idea in his head and — well, after a while he had me half-convinced. Wondering if maybe it would work."

Kelso said, "I guess it has worked before."

She gave him a sharp glance. "Listen, I'm not a whore. Sure, I work in a saloon. I help Emory sell his rotten liquor, and I entertain his customers by singing, because I've got a fair voice. But I don't go any further than that. You understand?"

He returned her stare for a long moment. Then he nodded. He wanted, strangely, to believe her. Why not, he thought. It could well be the truth. "No offense meant," he said.

As though she hadn't heard him, she went on. "I was raised on a small ranch. I know what a hard scrabble life it is for a woman. I ran away when I was old enough because I hated it. Well, I could never go back after being what I've become. But I would if I could."

"You were going to try it with Lynch?"

She thought a long time before she spoke. Finally, she said. "I don't know. I was tempted. It was a way out, you understand? And he was a good-looking man, in spite of the hard life he led when he was young, being a slave of the Comanches. You know about that?"

"I heard," Kelso said.

Briefly, she almost smiled. "He was vain as any Indian when it came to his looks," she said. "I used to wonder if those Comanche girls took to him."

"Jealous?"

"Are you crazy? I never was in love with Sam."

"But he was with you?"

"That's the way he was," she said. "What could I do about it?"

They picked their way eastward across the Panhandle, now and then fording a creek, the crossings road-plain, firm spots in the bottoms marked by the scattered settlers of the region. Kelso knew there could be quicksand in some of these meager streams.

One of the rangers, George Simon, gray and grizzled and ten years older than Kelso, rode up beside him and said, "When I joined up with this outfit, Sarge, they told me you was tough and calloused as all get hell. I never figured you as one for nurse-maiding much." There was no sarcasm in his words, just wonder. "You ever know this poor bastard before?"

"No. Just say I hope to beat those Comanches out of one. I hated the bastards when they were running wild, and I hate them worse when they use the reservation as a refuge to raid from."

"Know the feeling," Simon said. "But I thought maybe you was hoping to save him for that woman friend of his. Sort of playing cupid maybe."

Kelso said, "I talked to the girl. The feeling was all on Lynch's side!" The words came out stronger than he intended.

Simon gave him a strange look. "Well, well," he said.

"What the hell does that mean?"

"I don't rightly know. You wouldn't be taken up by that piece of fluff, your own self, now would you?"

"Only seen her less than an hour," Kelso said.

Simon shrugged. "Man gets the itch, his mind gets some peculiar ideas. Especially at your age."

"How the hell would you know?"

"I was young once myself."

"Thirty is a mite old for young," Kelso said.

"Hell of a lot younger than forty."

Kelso was silent for a moment, then he said, "You know, George, this life — being rangers — it ain't much."

"I'm too old to change," George said.

"Yeah, maybe. But me, maybe I'm not. Been thinking on it for some time. Dammit! I want a wife. A woman of my own, not just a quick roll with a whore in a back room somewhere, and months apart. Yeah, I might even take to raising young 'uns."

Simon was silent in turn. "Was a time I felt that way, too," he said finally. "But I let it slip away. You still got time, maybe, Sarge. If so, I wish you luck."

Kelso nodded. "What I'm saying — thinking like I been doing — well, that makes me sympathize with this poor bastard and what he wanted to do. I mean, with the girl and all."

"And the girl?"

Kelso shrugged. "Her, I ain't quite sure about. Seemed like the feeling between them was mostly one-sided."

"Never can tell about a woman," Simon said. He paused. "Maybe that's why I give up the idea."

With the arrow out of him, Lynch slept most of the time. This was a relief to Kelso and the other rangers who now rode without having to hear his moaning. Every time Kelso looked close at him, though, it seemed he looked more and more like a cadaver.

It was impossible to feed the wounded man, and only once in a while could they force a little water down his throat without choking him.

Four days later they rode into the ranger headquarters at Jacksboro. There were a few off-duty rangers there, and these came spilling out of their barracks as they spotted the escort.

Kelso didn't waste any time in explanations. He said, "Get Doc Nichols — fast!"

Nichols was an above-average medico who had attached himself to the ranger battalion when it was organized three years before. He was a long-time friend of Major John B. James, the battalion commander, but why he chose to take a job at a ranger's meager pay instead of continuing his practice in Austin, nobody seemed to know. Nobody asked. A man's reasons for joining the Texas Rangers were considered his own, so long as he performed his job well, and this Doc Nichols did.

Now he strode to the wagon and stood there staring, a middle-aged man as lean and leathery as the younger men around him. Only a great shock of white hair set him apart.

He saw the bandage on Lynch's head. "Scalped?"

Kelso nodded. "And a Comanche arrow clear through him."

"How long ago?"

"Four or five days."

Nichols shook his head in slow thoughtfulness.

Kelso saw this and said, "You got to save him, Doc."

Nichols looked at him curiously. "Friend of yours?"

"No. But I want to cheat those goddam Comanches out of this one."

"In that case," Nichols said, "I better get to work."

Chapter 2

It was June when the lone horseman rode down the dusty street of Bonner, two o'clock of a hot afternoon, with the sun glare making of him a nondescript dark blotch in the roadway, only one thing striking about his appearance. That thing was his hat. A new, light tan, flat-crowned, wide-brimmed California style John B. Stetson, a startling contrast to his hard-used range clothes and the unprepossessing dun mount he rode.

Rademacher, the barber, was likely the first person in Bonner to take notice, sitting idle in one of his two chairs, the other empty, waiting for customers and wondering, at first, if this might be one.

His squint of curiosity gave way to open-eyed surprise, and he bounded up to cross to the fronting window and stare. "By God!" he said. "By *God!*"

He rushed outside, but the rider had continued down the street toward Emory's saloon. Rademacher started after him, walking fast,

26

then hesitated as he came even with Murdock's store. He turned then and plunged into the mercantile. "He's alive and back," he said. "It's Lynch!"

Murdock came out of the interior gloom to join him under the portico as they watched the rider dismount in front of the saloon.

"Christ!" Murdock said. "He survived! I never would have bet on his chances."

"Reckon he's headed first off to see Annie," Rademacher said.

"Don't look no worse for wear, what I can see."

"Yeah, don't look no different."

"Got a new hat, is all."

"Well, he ain't been prosperous, convalescing from his wounds," Murdock said. "Ain't likely he could afford a complete new outfit, now, is it?"

"Hey! I wonder how — I mean, the way them Comanches lifted his hair and all —"

"Yeah," Murdock said. "Could be somewhat of a shocker for Annie, couldn't it?"

"Hell of a thing," Rademacher said. "Hell of a thing."

"Yeah, it could be that."

They stood there then, staring down the street in silence.

Lynch reached the saloon and sat his saddle, not dismounting.

Still, he had to know. It was the reason he had come back to Bonner after all these months of roaming, months after he had left the ranger doctor's care.

He had traded off the team and wagon the rangers had used to bring him in, and he had bought a horse and saddle, and then he had ridden slowly, living like an Indian himself and brooding. Until now, finally, he was at Emory's place where Annie worked and sometimes sang as Emory's star attraction.

Well, now he would find out, he thought. He swung down and tied his reins to the hitchrack.

At that moment Annie came out of the saloon, and Lynch stood silent and unmoving as she did not notice him, her face turned away toward the man who followed her.

He was a blocky figure of a man, solid on his feet, dressed as a cowboy. He was in his thirties, coarsely handsome, with heavy, ruddy features and a thick blonde cavalry mustache and long sideburns. As he exited the batwing doors, he reached out and grabbed Annie's arm so that she cried out in pain.

"Hold on, now, girl," he said, grinning. "I only want to talk to you."

"I've heard all your kind of talk I can stand," she said.

"You must have heard my kind of talk before," he said. "A man needs a woman like you, now and then. Don't get high and mighty with old Cole Rutledge, you've heard it all, girl."

"Not addressed to me, I haven't," she said. "Not till you came along."

"Hell, that's what Emory keeps you around for, ain't it? To make conversation with lonely men so they'll buy his likker."

"I sing and I dance," she said angrily. "That's all."

"Why, hell, that's pure waste. I bet you got other talents that could please a man more." Rutledge jerked her suddenly against his chest and shoved his face down against hers. But he did not kiss her. Instead, he raked his brush of a mustache hard across her mouth and cheek, leaving a reddening swatch of bruised skin.

She was in her dance hall dress, and unhampered by her street clothing. She slammed her knee up hard into his groin. He doubled in agony, and she clawed her nails at his jaw and drew blood.

"Goddam you!" he said.

She turned then to get away from him, and saw Lynch standing there. Lynch had a sixgun in his hand and was holding it leveled with Rutledge's belly.

Rutledge straightened from his hurt and saw the gun and said, "Hold on now, friend! Me and Annie was just playing around. It's a kind of a game."

"The game is over," Lynch said.

For a long moment Rutledge looked like a cougar about to spring. Then he stared into Lynch's eyes and something he saw there changed his mind. He made himself smile. "Didn't know Annie was a friend of yours," he said. "My apologies, if that is so."

"More than a friend," Lynch said. "We was figuring to get married."

Rutledge looked surprised, but he said, "Well now, that does make a difference. Friend, you and her both got my apology."

"You'd best go back inside," Lynch said. "And don't ever grab her that way again."

Rutledge stopped smiling. He met Lynch's stare for a long time. Then, abruptly, he said, "So be it," and turned and went back in.

Annie cried out to Lynch and ran down the steps toward him. "Sam!" She held out her hand to him.

He took it in his, hesitated, then drew her into his arms.

For a short time she stayed unmoving, then raised her palms to push away and look up into his face. She said, "You are looking well," and felt him stiffen.

He said, "Can we go somewhere and talk?"

"I'll tell Emory," she said. She went back into the saloon. Almost at once she reappeared.

They walked toward the edge of town, and she kept glancing covertly at him, studying the wan look of his cheek, the stubborn set of his jaw, the bitter line of his lips.

She said, "Do you feel well, Sam?"

"Well enough," he said.

"What does that mean?"

"Well enough, considering the butchering them Comanches gave me."

A shadow crossed her face. She seemed about to speak, hesitated, then remained silent.

The last structure of the town was behind them now, and she stopped. He stopped, too, and turned back to face her.

"Things may not be the same between us as they was," he said.

"Of course they will be."

He gave a single shake of his head, but said nothing.

"What is it, Sam?"

"What do you think it is?"

A quick horror showed in her eyes. "They didn't — The Comanches — they didn't — I mean, your manhood —"

31

"Geld me? No. But maybe they might as well have."

"Sam!"

"I reckon things might sometimes change between a man and a woman," he said. He reached up and swept off his hat.

The shock was too much for her to hide.

"Now you know," he said.

She hated herself for what her face had revealed to him.

"I guess they might as well have gelded me," he said. "You don't have to try to hide your feelings."

"But, Sam, you've always misunderstood my feelings from the start. We have never been more than friends."

"You don't have to lie to me," he said. His face was hard.

She knew the hardness hid a deep, deep hurt, and her eyes filled with tears at what she was doing to him. Her voice was no more than a whisper. "I'm telling you true, Sam. Please believe me. This has nothing to do with it."

"You can fool yourself, maybe," he said. "But you can't fool me."

"No!"

"We were going to get married," he said.

"I never promised any such thing!"

"But you would have. I know you would have."

"Oh, Sam. Please. No! I never felt that way about you. If I had, this wouldn't change anything."

"You go ahead and keep believing that," he said. "It will make it easier on you."

"It isn't that," she said. "Sam, believe me, it isn't that."

He put his hat back on. "I got one thing left to do," he said slowly. "I'm going to kill every goddam Comanche I can find."

Chapter 3

It was August when Major John B. James called Kelso into his meagerly furnished office.

He looked up from his battered desk and nodded.

Kelso had just ridden in from another assignment and was tired. He didn't salute. The major didn't expect him to. The Texas Rangers were only loosely organized along military lines. There was no spit and polish to them.

James said, "Sit down, John," and gestured to a straight-backed chair.

Kelso sat, first turning the chair around to straddle it and resting his arms across the back of it. He and the major were both dressed in typical range garb. The rangers didn't wear uniforms or rank insignia.

The major stared at Kelso for a while, as if he were getting his thoughts together. James seldom spoke without thinking. He was well respected because of that.

Finally he said, "There's been some trouble lately up on the Cache Creek reservation."

34

"That's Fort Sill," Kelso said. "Injun Territory. The U.S. Army's job."

The major nodded. He was silent again before he went on. Then he said, "You ever wonder what happened to Sam Lynch?"

"Of course," Kelso said. "It was me that brought him in last year three-quarters dead, remember?"

James said, "Well, it took him a while to fully recover, I reckon. Though he was only under Doc's care for a few weeks before he up and disappeared and Doc or none of the rest of us ever saw him again."

"He was tough," Kelso said, remembering. "But maybe he didn't survive after all."

"We're sure he did."

"Sure? Why?"

"This past month there's been four Comanche braves scalped right on the Cache Creek Agency. All were Comanches of the Kwahadi band."

Kelso let a long silence hang between them before he spoke. "You think Sam did it?"

"Not only me. The agent at Cache, name of Hart, has some evidence to indicate it. And the commanding officer at Fort Sill, Colonel Richardson, agrees with him."

"What evidence? Just because some Comanches get themselves killed and scalped —"

"Not always killed first," the major said.

"Two of them were only wounded, shot from ambush, but all were scalped. The two wounded died later, but only after they identified their attacker as a white man."

"Damned careless of him," Kelso said. "He should have made sure."

James shook his head. "My guess is he wanted it that way. He wanted the Comanches to know who he was. He even took off his hat and pointed at his own scarred head to make sure they knew."

"It does sound like Lynch, maybe. Well, he had good reason."

"The point is, Kelso, it's against federal law to kill reservation Injuns."

"So why don't the federal law or the Army catch him?"

"They've been trying. They've combed the Injun Territory looking. And they tracked him into the Panhandle, then lost his trail."

"Cavalry wouldn't be stopped by the Texas border," Kelso said. "Nor the federal deputy marshals, neither."

The major nodded. "The trouble is, the deputy marshals got all they can handle up there in the Territory. They're short of manpower. And the Army — well, hell! can you just see a Army patrol ever running down a lone Texan in Texas?"

Kelso said, "Nor a ranger patrol, neither.

36

Not if Lynch is as Injun-wise as he seems to be."

James got up and walked out from behind his desk and paced across the room and back. He remained standing and said, "He's Injun-wise, all right. As much so almost as a Comanche himself. No bunch of white men is going to catch him. One white man might."

After a long hesitation, Kelso said, "Me? No, thanks, Major. I was the one to find him there laying in his own blood with his hair lifted, and I like to think I saved his life. I won't be the one that brings him in to stand trial for killing Comanches. Not after what they did to him."

The major frowned. "When you joined the Rangers you took an oath not to let personal considerations interfere with doing your job."

When Kelso said nothing, he went on, "I need you on this one, John. You're as trail-wise a man as I've got. Probably the best rifle shot. You might be able to wing him where somebody else would have to kill him. You wouldn't want to see him brought in dead?"

"I don't want to see him brought in at all. I'd rather see him go on killing Comanches."

"Then think of this. If a white man doesn't find him, the Comanches will. Already, I hear,

37

a bunch have jumped the Agency to go hunting for him."

Kelso said, "Better them than me."

James looked at him steadily and said, "I don't think you mean that. Think about it, John. Those are Kwahadies that jumped. Led by a troublemaker the whites call Piavah. Lynch's victims were all Kwahadies. You know what they'll do to him if they get him? Torture, slow agony, death by inches."

Kelso thought about this and it began to make a difference. But he said, "You're not wanting to send me out after him just to save him from being tortured. There's got to be another reason."

James took a while to answer. Then he said, "The real reason is this — and the colonel at Sill and the agent at Cache and the governor of Texas all agree — Sam Lynch may keep killing for a while, even with the Comanches after him. If he does, they're going to take their retaliation against any whites they come across. You have any idea how many settlers have poured into the Panhandle this past year? They're all sitting targets for marauding Comanches. Those red bastards start tasting white blood again, they won't stop. Your goddam friend Lynch will turn the Panhandle into a Comanche slaughterhouse."

Kelso sat in silence, getting a picture of this

in his mind, seeing the whole of northwest Texas set on fire by one man. Why the hell did Lynch have to do this? he thought. Then he said, "When do you want me to leave?"

Chapter 4

Lynch was watching when Piavah's bunch left the reservation. He had been watching for days, hanging around the fringes of the Cache Creek Agency, staying out of sight after his last killing and scalping of a luckless brave, pulling back many miles to hunt the small game and antelope on which he existed, but always returning to take up his vigil.

Lynch had known they would jump again, because he knew Piavah. Oh, God! how he knew Piavah. The horses he had tended all those years he had been held by the Comanches had belonged to Piavah's father, a sometimes war chief. Lynch had hated Piavah worst of all. Piavah was a spoiled-rotten young buck only a couple of years older than Lynch. And the sonofabitch had got his kicks out of making Lynch's life as miserable as possible.

At that, Lynch had been lucky. Some of the young captive slaves, especially Mexican boys, were gelded to make them docile. It was mostly whim that decided how the Comanches treated their captives.

The Comanches, in those days, could not have maintained their huge horse herds without using their captives as horsetenders. Not if they were going to spend all of their own time hunting and raiding and making war.

Lynch knew he had been a fool to come back and settle in the Panhandle even after Quanah had given up and brought the last of the hold-out Comanches to the reservation and adopted the white man's way himself.

But Lynch had known of that good spot for his horse ranch. And he knew how to breed and raise horses. That was one thing he had learned during his slavery with the Kwahadies. They were the greatest horsemen of the plains. And Lynch had convinced himself the depredations were over and he had taken his chance.

He had forgotten how it was with the young buck Comanches. Without war there was no way for a Comanche brave to gain prestige. He should have known there would always be young bucks eager to rape and pillage and kill for kicks and glory.

Well, he would never forget again. He took off his Stetson and fingered the great lumps of scar tissue which covered his skull.

He was lying now in a thicket of blackjack on a bluff above the Red River as Piavah led

41

his band of maybe forty braves across. Lynch put his hat back on and his mouth tightened into a hard smile. It was working the way he had planned. He had known his attack on the Kwahadi braves on the Agency ground would drive Piavah to seek retaliation. Lynch had deliberately left trail signs all the way to the Panhandle, then come back by a different route to watch them follow. It had been too dangerous to keep attacking on the reserve among the hundreds of Comanches, and with the Army right there at Sill. But once he had drawn the renegades back into Texas he would wage his one-man vendetta on his own terms. He would get every one of Piavah's bunch. It was a vow he had made to himself.

He had been willing to forget his captive treatment, once he had escaped them. For eight years he had been willing to forget, and had gone about his peaceful way making his living as a wrangler and sometimes bronc rider, mostly in central Texas, till he got a stake and figured it was time to strike out on his own. And then, with his ranch established for over a year, Piavah had suddenly appeared like something out of a bad dream.

Lynch had recognized the bastard just before he'd taken the arrow in his chest and felt the hacking of the tomahawk at his scalp before he passed out from the pain.

He wondered now if Piavah had recognized *him* after all those years. Not that it mattered. Lynch would always know Piavah when he saw him. Piavah hadn't changed much. The cruel, sullen face had broadened with maturity, but the black demented eyes were the same.

Maybe he would save Piavah for the last, Lynch thought. He would kill Piavah's men, one by one, first. Lynch's hard smile returned. That was what he lived for now. There was nothing else for him now but that. Nothing else he wanted except revenge for his mutilation.

Some of it had to do with Annie, the way she had taken his appearance when he'd gone back to Bonner after he'd left Doc Nichols' care.

Some of it went back to before his scalping, of course. It went back to when he was twelve, to when the Comanches had swept in and murdered his parents and raped his sister to death.

He had tried to forget all that, and maybe he could have if it hadn't all come back, all the dormant hate and lust for their blood when he saw the way Annie looked at him after he'd been cut up . . .

Piavah had guessed by now that the vengeance-crazed white man who had assaulted

43

his braves was the one he had thought they'd killed at the horse ranch. He had not recognized the rancher then, but now he recalled there was something vaguely familiar about him.

It had only been by chance that he'd led the raid on the ranch. It had been because of how the last buffalo hunt turned out.

Three and a half years of reservation life had left the Comanches discontented and resentful. Quanah had taken the white man's way, but wasn't he half-white himself? Wasn't his mother the white woman captive Cynthia Parker? True, Quanah, the half-breed, had become one of the great Comanche war chiefs for a while. But when he went onto the reservation, he adopted the white man's role and adapted easily to it. For the others it was not that easy. Quanah had been a Comanche for thirty years. The Comanches, as a people, went back eight thousand years.

They sat idle and restless at Cache Creek and grumbled over the government hand-out of two or three pounds of beef per week, which left them always hungry, and they thought about the great herds of buffalo that ranged the Panhandle, which for centuries had been their private preserve. And they lay shivering in winter in the thin government-issue blankets, and they thought about the warm buffalo robes to which they had been accustomed.

Because a few braves like Piavah had stolen horses when, in the beginning, they had been let off the reservation to hunt, the passes had been revoked and the Army had adamantly refused their pleas to seek food for themselves.

Then a new agent came to the Cache Creek Agency. His name was Hart, and he was naive yet. He was shocked at the conditions he found, and he argued for the Comanches and finally convinced the Army commander to once again grant them hunting passes.

The Army agreed to let all go who wanted to go, on a single great hunt in that fall of '78. A small military escort would go with them.

The Comanches quickly shed their discontent and resurrected the buffalo dances, and the old men suddenly came to life and retold stories of earlier great hunts and prepared themselves for this new one, and instructed the young boys in how it was.

Their enthusiasm was so great that it infected Agent Hart and even the soldiers of the escort. The soldiers had feared and hated the Comanches as an enemy, but now that they were subdued, some hated to see them hungry.

On the appointed day fifteen hundred Comanches rode west from Fort Sill, escorted by a troop of cavalry. So abject had most of the Comanches become that the soldiers had no fear of the odds. And of the fifteen hundred, more than half were women and children. The women would do much of the skinning and butchering and all of the cooking, and the braves would be free for the hunting which all expected to be great.

The Comanches sent out braves to scout ahead for the buffalo, and they studied the skies for smoke signs which would tell them the buffalo had been found. No signals came, and the scouts came in and ate and went out again. And so went the first days of the hunt.

The scouts came back and reported nothing and went out again and again. The second day went like the first and the third went like the second. And the fourth. And on the fifth day the scouts rode back and said they had found great scatterings of bleached buffalo bones.

And now the whole fifteen hundred were into the Panhandle and they looked for themselves. At first they thought a fall of snow had come early to the plain. But then, as they got closer, they saw not snow but a thick layer of white skulls and skeletons of slaughtered herds. The carpet of bones extended as far as their eyes could see. The bones were all they had been left by the white hide-hunters.

Now the disgruntled ones began to say there

were no buffalo left, that there would be no meat for the winter, no robes. They said the scant issue rations were almost gone and that the expedition should turn back.

Piavah was not one of these. He gathered around him a cluster of young braves like himself, and they held their own council which did not include the old men. Piavah said they should strike south and outrun the soldiers and go to Mexico if they had to, to be free.

The old men also held a council. They believed what they wanted to believe and tried to convince one another. The old men told each other that the herds would come as soon as the weather got colder. That the buffalo would come down from the north to winter graze as they had always come. The old men told this to the other Comanches, and most of them believed it for the same reason that the old men believed it.

But when the frost lay on the grass, there were still no herds. The old men got out their buffalo medicine and prayed, but nothing came except a first, light snow. The women began to urge their men to turn back; their children were crying with hunger.

The hunting pass expired. The escort troop captain ignored this fact, and his eyes searched the horizon as ceaselessly as those of the Comanches. He did not understand his own feel-

47

ing, but he understood the feeling of the Comanches.

Some of the squaws convinced their men, and the families began to desert the expedition, making their way back toward the miserable security of the Agency.

A heavier snow fell and the Comanches had to kill some of their horses for food.

The agent, Hart, received the first straggling deserters and learned of the predicament of the rest. He sent out wagons of rice and flour, which was all he had to send them.

The Comanches heard the wagons coming and came out of their tipis where they had taken refuge from another snow storm. They took the rice and the flour and were kept from starving, but they knew now that there were no buffalo left in the Panhandle. In the few years since they had left, the white hide-hunters had killed off the herds.

The camp was struck and the Comanches rode and walked beside the wagons returning to the reservation, saddened and bitter.

Beside them rode the soldiers and the soldiers' captain, and they were somehow sad and bitter, too.

The bitterness of the soldiers was two-edged, because sometime during the storm Piavah and a dozen braves had disappeared, their tracks leading south.

But the captain's orders were to escort the hunting party and made no provision for pursuing dissenting renegades. He could only hope that Piavah's desertion would be a temporary thing. He did not know, of course, that Piavah would chance upon an isolated horse ranch and scalp alive the rancher, the man called Sam Lynch, before unpredictably leading the deserters back to the Agency.

Chapter 5

A couple of days after Kelso got his orders from Major James, he rode into the Cache Creek Agency and found Agent Hart.

The agent was a tall, thin, middle-aged man with a creased, worried, but friendly face. And he was distraught.

As soon as Kelso introduced himself, he said, "Piavah's gone again. And this time he's taken forty braves with him."

Kelso said, "What's being done?"

"Nothing."

"No cavalry after him?"

Hart shook his head. "Colonel Richardson refuses to send out any. I think he's hoping the Comanches catch Lynch out there and put an end to the trouble he's caused here on the reservation." He hesitated, then went on, "The cavalry couldn't catch Piavah anyway. His braves took along spare horses, the way they always do. When one horse tires, they jump onto another. No way a heavy-mounted cavalry troop could overtake them."

"I'll be getting on," Kelso said.

"What can one ranger do against them?"

"I'm not after the Comanches. I'm after Lynch."

Hart said, "That's right. I was forgetting. But if Piavah's braves start marauding out there —"

"If I get Lynch, maybe they'll stop."

"You mean give him up to them?"

Kelso said, "Hell, no!"

Hart said uneasily, "It was just a thought. It might save the lives of some innocent settlers."

Kelso said, slow and hard, "I hope you don't mean that. So I'm going to forget you said it. There is nothing would ever make me turn a white man over to those Comanche bastards."

Hart nodded slowly. "When I took this job as Indian Agent, I didn't know what I was getting into. Indians are like children, really. They live by whim and impulse and they have no real concept of right and wrong. They can turn vicious in a minute, change from amiable children to murderous savages, and they have a love of cruelty that turns me sick. I am not a Quaker like my predecessor, and I came here with a fair amount of cynicism. But I'd never believed the stories of Comanche cruelty until I witnessed some of it myself." He paused, then added, "But, of course, I've never seen them torture a captive."

Kelso said, "You got to remember that to them war and killing has always been a game. No Comanche ever wanted peace. Peace bores them. Hell, before the white man came they were killing and torturing other Injuns."

"I cannot argue what you say," Hart said. "Yet I have some sympathy for them."

"I haven't. Not after what they did to Lynch last year."

"A terrible thing. I'll never understand these people."

Kelso said, "Well, you aren't alone."

Hart said, "I've tried to study them. I've read what I could find written about them, which isn't much. Did you know that they were once Shoshones and cousins to the Utes, and lived in the Rockies? That was a long time ago according to their old men. The Utes called them *Coh-mats,* or something like that. It means 'Those Who Are Always Against Us.' "

"Ornery bastards, even then," Kelso said.

"They split away from the other Shoshones and migrated down to the plains and found them full of wild horses as well as buffalo. They took instantly to the horses and became the greatest riders of all the Indians. And the greatest raiders."

"There aren't any Texans would argue that," Kelso said. "But I run onto a few Shoshone and I never would have believed they were the same breed of animal."

"You've got to remember this all happened over a period of two hundred years or more."

"And they're still as ornery as ever," Kelso said.

Hart said, "There is something else to remember — about this one we call Piavah. A few years back he probably wouldn't have any followers. He is known among the Comanches as a *pukutsi*, which translates into something like an eccentric. But he is a good orator and a firebrand and he apparently sees himself as a war chief. So he is a dangerous man."

"Any Comanche on the loose is dangerous," Kelso said. "I think I'll ride to the Fort and talk some to that colonel."

Kelso reined up in front of the Fort Sill headquarters with a pretty fair idea of how the colonel would receive him. There was considerable hard feeling between the Army and the Rangers because of the former federal policy of letting Indians go into Texas to hunt. All Texans resented this, and a lot of rangers were inclined to shoot the hunters on sight. This infuriated the Army brass. And although the hunting passes were not being issued any more, the mutual bitterness lingered.

Colonel Richardson was a small, wiry man who had been a brevet major-general in the Civil War. He did not hide his belligerency.

He said to Kelso, "I've no intention of chasing after those jumping braves. If it weren't for that murdering Texan killing them here on the reservation, there wouldn't be any trouble. I hope he tries it again out there and they get him. Once that's done, I'll see that Piavah is brought back here."

"Might be hard to do by then," Kelso said. "Piavah gets a taste of blood out there, he may get a big thirst for more."

"I'll take care of that, if the time comes. I don't need any Texan Johnny Reb advising me."

"I just wanted to know your position," Kelso said. "Or any information you might want to give. The War is long over, Colonel."

Richardson's antagonism lessened slightly. He said, "Well, there are troops in the Panhandle now. Not mine, but those of Lieutenant-Colonel Davids at Fort Elliott. He has the Tenth Cavalry there. That's more than a hundred miles north of the town of Bonner, but he has patrols out frequently. It's possible he'll run onto those bronco Comanches. However,

I'll repeat my own hope that the broncos catch that murdering Texan first."

"Do you know what they did to him, Colonel?"

"Yes, I've heard. And he lived. He should consider himself lucky that he did. Only a damn fool or a madman would come back risking his neck for more."

"I reckon what they did to him would make most any man mad," Kelso said.

"I mean crazy mad," the colonel said.

"That, too," Kelso said, thoughtfully. It was something to think about. It made him wonder if Lynch had gone mad the way the colonel meant. It could happen, he supposed.

Chapter 6

Once free of the reservation, and having discovered by sending scouts to his rear that no soldiers had taken up his trail, Piavah felt his medicine grow strong. So strong, in fact, that he made an impulsive decision to continue on to Mexico.

Piavah knew that Lynch was following, but he saw no reason to waste time hunting the scalp-taker. He would simply wait until Lynch made another attack and he would somehow catch him then. He might lose another brave or two, but that did not overly concern him.

On the other hand, to make a Moon Raid into Mexico as the old war chiefs had done for two hundred years — that would be an achievement. There had been no such raid since before the surrender by Quanah, whom Piavah now considered a traitor to his people.

When the Comanches on the reservation heard Piavah had led a Moon Raid, he would be a big man. It would be Piavah they remembered, not Quanah.

Piavah had gone on the last Moon Raid of his people, before Quanah capitulated to Mackenzie. He had been only sixteen at the time, but he remembered it as the finest event of his life.

And now he would lead his own raiders, and his heart sang at the thought.

He would follow the old Comanche Trail, as he remembered it. He knew it would lead him down through the Panhandle and across the river that the *Tejanos* and the Mexicans called the Pecos, and through the Big Bend of the river they called the Bravo or the Rio Grande.

There was still rich raiding to be had in Mexico, horses to steal, women to rape, enough to make a Comanche warrior's blood sing.

And there was always the time ahead when the *taybay-boh,* the white man called Lynch, would come too close, like a moth to a torch, and Piavah would have him. Piavah had special plans for the scalp-taker when that time came. He would make the killing of Lynch last a long time — two, perhaps three days of torture. Just thinking about what he would do to Lynch made him feel happy. This was the good life, now that he was free again, away from the miserable confinement of the reservation. With the livestock to steal and the women to take, and the *taybay-boh* to torture, it all made a Comanche feel like he had a future again. The way it was meant for a Comanche to feel. It made a man feel good, and clean and wholesome inside.

Kelso followed the trail on a tiring horse, cursing himself now because he realized Lynch was leading a spare mount. He must be, because he was keeping up with Piavah's bunch, and Kelso was falling behind each day — he could tell that by their tracks. Still, because he traveled light, unencumbered by the heavy equipment which was standard for the cavalry, he could keep on.

His horse was a mustang mount which had mostly lived on grass, like the Comanche horses, chosen because it had seldom known grain, unlike the Army mounts.

This was a trick some Texas Rangers had learned early. And to bolster his slim rations, he shot small game now and then. He was, as Major James had mentioned, an exceptional shot with a rifle.

It bothered him that he was being outdistanced by Lynch. He should have known that a man who had lived with the Comanches would have learned from them, and would have adopted their way of traveling with spare horses.

★ ★ ★

Sam Lynch, in fact, had two spare horses, one of which he had just taken when he killed the last scout sent back by Piavah to spy on him. Sam had known they would be checking on him, and he had neatly ambushed the Indian, scalped him and taken his horse.

The main body of the Comanches was far ahead, but that was because he wanted it that way. He liked the way things were going and hoped that Piavah would send back more lone warriors. They were grist for his mill, he thought. One by one he would get them all if this kept up. But, of course, he knew it wouldn't. Piavah would soon realize this was a mistake.

Well, he would follow them no matter where their trail led, and he would wait for his opportunities. He guessed now that Piavah was planning to raid into Mexico. That suited Lynch just fine. Let them raid successfully, and when they were burdened down with loot and livestock and captive women, they would be vulnerable to his attacks.

He would have to be careful, of course. He intended to be just that. He didn't mind dying — not since he'd seen Annie the last time. But he was terrified of dying by torture at their hands. That was what they would want

— to take him alive and to stick greasewood splinters into his flesh and set them on fire, to remove his eyelids and stake him out on an anthill, or to cut off his genitals. That was just for openers.

Sam Lynch knew of their other refinements in the art of torture — he had been forced to watch them torture other captives while he was their slave. The Comanches had enjoyed watching his revulsion almost as much as they had enjoyed watching their victims' agonies.

Oh, they were a caution, the Comanches were. They loved their fun and games.

It was likely that Kelso would have lost them all if Piavah had not suddenly and inexplicably swerved eastward off the trail. Although he could not pick out Lynch's tracks in the welter of Comanche pony prints, Kelso figured Lynch would not be far behind them. He had not followed many miles when the thought struck him that the town of Bonner was not far ahead. Kelso began to swear. Piavah, it appeared, was going to have some sport right now. He wasn't going to wait for it until he got to Mexico or wherever it was he was headed. He was going to detour slightly and give his braves something to wet their blood lust.

Just thinking about what forty Comanches could do to the little town brought the sweat out on Kelso's face.

And thinking about this he rode right into the trap they had set.

There were four of them, all young bucks and looking meaner than hell. One of them had black curly hair instead of straight, and this meant he was surely a breed, probably half-Mexican. Some Mex girl captive's bastard, Kelso thought. The Comanches would have raised him to be a brave, with the same rights as a full-blood.

The breed Comanche said, in Spanish, "Do not try for your gun."

Kelso looked at four carbines pointed at him, weighed the possibilities, and shook his head. He answered in the same lingo, "For sure."

"You are *Tejano*. You are ranger," the breed said. "Why do you follow us?"

"I do not follow you. I follow the one who follows you."

"The one who hunts our scalps?" the breed said.

"The same. The one called Lynch."

"Why should you follow him?"

"He is wanted by the Father of the *Tejanos* because he takes your scalps. He is to be punished for that."

61

The breed's face showed bewilderment, then disbelief.

"You lie. Since when does one *Tejano* punish another for killing Comanches?"

"I tell you how it is," Kelso said simply.

The breed said something in Comanche, and one of the braves rode forward and took Kelso's Colt from his holster and his carbine from its saddle scabbard.

"Piavah will decide," the breed said.

"The *Tejanos* are trying to help you," Kelso said.

The breed snorted. "The *Tejanos* and the Comanches are enemies."

Kelso shrugged. "We are now at peace."

The breed Comanche showed his Mexican blood in the flash of his white teeth. "Tell that to Lynch, the scalp-hunter."

Kelso had no answer for that.

"*Siga,*" the breed said. "We go to talk to Piavah."

Kelso rode beside the breed, the other three fell in behind.

Kelso said, "You are curly-haired, so I will call you *Chino.*" In Mexican slang that was what *chino* meant.

The breed Comanche shrugged.

"Did you know Lynch from before?"

Chino said, "From before what?"

"He was once a captive of the Kwahadies."

"You know, then?" Chino's Spanish was not fluent. It was what you would expect from a half-breed born of a Mexican mother who had likely forgotten much of her own tongue, but who had imparted some of it to him while he was still a child. Also, trade-lingo Spanish had been used and passed on among the Comanches during the years of trade with the Comancheros, who were mostly Hispanic New Mexicans.

"You were heading south," Kelso said. "To Mexico? On a Moon Raid?"

"You talk too much," Chino said.

"Against your own people."

"I am Comanche," Chino said. "My people are the Kwahadies. I care nothing for Mexicans."

"What will you do in Bonner?"

"Bonner?"

"The pueblo up ahead. That is where Piavah is going, no?"

Chino said again, "Piavah will decide."

Kelso figured there was no use talking to him.

They entered a shallow canyon, on each side of which was a thrust of shale. Kelso was surprised that none of the Comanches rode as flankers. It appeared that three years or more of reservation life had taken the edge off their keenness.

The four fast rifle shots took their toll. Kelso reined up at the sound and held his mount close-checked, sitting rigid in his saddle. Behind him the three Comanches fell off their horses and lay still. Chino clapped a hand against his side, and blood spurted through his fingers as he kicked his own mount and fled at a run out of the swale onto the flat country beyond.

Kelso waited, turning his head to look, not turning his horse.

Then behind him he heard the voice. "Keep your hands in sight."

Kelso held up his hands where Lynch could see them. He was sure it was Lynch.

Lynch rode up and peered at him. "Yep," he said. "Kelso. I was pretty sure it was you."

Kelso started to drop his hands.

"Hold it!" Lynch studied Kelso's empty holster and rifle scabbard. "All right. I guess you ain't armed."

The ranger let his hands fall. He pointed to one of the dead Comanches. Kelso's sixgun was still shoved into the waistband of the brave's buckskin trousers, and his rifle lay where the brave had dropped it.

Lynch dismounted and picked the weapons up. He kept an eye on Kelso. "Don't try to ride off."

"After that exhibition of target shooting?"

64

Lynch got back into the saddle. "I been getting some practice lately."

"I heard."

Kelso studied him. He was a handsome man, the kind that women would find attractive, Kelso thought. He was wearing a flat-crowned, California-style hat which hid what had happened to his head.

Lynch said, "That why you're here?"

Kelso said, "While we're jawboning here, Piavah's bucks are heading straight for Bonner."

"We'll head there, too. But hold on, I damn near forgot something." Lynch got down from his saddle again, still holding Kelso's rifle. He laid it carefully on the ground, then went from one to the other of the dead Comanches. Kelso saw the glint of the scalping knife as he took his trophies.

Lynch straightened up, holding the three scalp locks in his left hand. Without looking at Kelso he went to a large, soft saddlebag hung on his rig and opened it and took out three hooked wire hoops and stretched the scalps on them. He tied the fresh scalps loose to a saddle thong so that they would dry in the sun and air.

He remounted and said, "We can ride now. But one other thing — I got a couple extra horses ground-hitched beyond that rise. Bet-

65

ter put your saddle on one of them, your own looks beat."

A few minutes later they were riding after the blood-spattered tracks of Chino, each leading a spare mount.

After a while, Lynch said, "Why you been following me?"

"Sam, you can't murder Injuns on a government reservation. It ain't legal."

"I been getting even," Lynch said. "You seen what they did to me."

"I saw."

"Yeah. And look at me now." Lynch swept off his hat.

Kelso felt his skin grow cold. Above Lynch's handsome face most of his head was a tortuous mass of white and pink scar tissue.

Lynch saw the quick-hidden, shocked revulsion in Kelso's eyes and said bitterly, "Yeah. Now you know how Annie feels." Then he said, "So there's nothing left for me except getting even." He put his hat back on.

Kelso didn't know what else to say, so he said, "It's still against the law, Sam."

"They ain't on the reservation now," Lynch said.

"You led them off, Sam."

"Sure."

"And now they're going to hit Bonner,"

66

Kelso said. "Those people were your friends."

"Yeah." Lynch's face showed a deep concern. He said, "And Annie is there."

Kelso rode without commenting on this.

After a long silence, Lynch said, "Goddammit! It wasn't my intention to stir the red bastards up to raiding again."

"Things got a way of getting out of hand," Kelso said.

Lynch brooded on this awhile. Then he said, "I never got the chance to thank you proper for keeping me alive last year. I owe you for it."

"You surprised me, leaving Doc Nichols' care so soon."

"I couldn't just lay there thinking about it. There was things I had to find out. Like what was left of my ranch and where Piavah could be found — did you know I knew the bastard from when I was a kid captive?"

"Heard something on it."

A long quiet hung between them. Then Lynch said, "There was another thing I had to find out about, too."

"What's that?" Kelso said, when Lynch did not go on.

"Maybe you'll find out when we get to Bonner."

"If Piavah's bunch doesn't wipe it out."

"Let's hope there's some ranchers in town.

Maybe enough to beat the bastards off,"
Lynch said.

"Let's hope," Kelso said. Unconsciously, he
kicked his horse and it broke into a lope. It
was a poor pace for the led horses, and he
soon dropped back to a walk. "Two men
won't make much difference," he said.

Lynch pulled up reluctantly. "It might,"
he said. But he matched Kelso's pace. "On
the other hand, the horses are important."

"My thinking," Kelso said. Then, "Best
give me back my guns."

Lynch studied him. "Truce until this thing
at Bonner is over?"

"Truce," Kelso said.

Lynch handed over the weapons. "What
you think they'd do to me, was you to bring
me in?"

Kelso shook his head. "Don't rightly know.
You'll have to stand trial for murder, I reckon.
Be up to a jury how it comes out."

"Texas jury?"

"Maybe. It's the Texas governor's orders
to bring you in. Hard to say if maybe a federal
court can't wangle jurisdiction somehow."

"If it was Texans on the jury it wouldn't
make no difference," Lynch said. "No Texan
jury would convict a white man for killing
Comanches."

"Likely not."

"But if I was taken in, it would put a crimp into me getting even with the red bastards."

Kelso said, "The way I see it, you're way ahead of the game. You got — what? — eight of their scalps?"

"That's one way to figure, maybe," Lynch said. "But not my way. I want to kill every one of Piavah's bunch that scalped me." He reached for his hat again. "Take another look."

Kelso did not turn his head. "Never mind."

"Now you know how a woman would feel," Lynch said.

There it was again, Kelso thought. He said, "We got a truce, let's forget it for now. The big thing now is what Piavah's doing at Bonner.

An hour later they found out. Piavah had treed the town. From a low rise two miles away, they could see Piavah's Comanches hidden at strategic cover in the brush surrounding Bonner.

"Wonder if those townsfolk know they're there?" Kelso said.

"They will damn soon. Comanches don't like to wait. They don't have the patience of an Apache. I'm surprised they didn't just ride up and attack."

"Must be a reason."

"Looks like a lot of horses and wagons on

the main street. And that means there are settlers come to town."

Kelso said, "Maybe they got the Comanches outnumbered."

"Maybe." Lynch was thoughtful, then he said, "You got to remember that Piavah ain't a experienced war chief. He went along on a few raids before Quanah gave up, and since then his life has been blanket Injun. Might be he is still trying to figure out how to handle this."

"Makes sense. All them wagons could have surprised him."

"He'll have to decide soon, though," Lynch said. "Those braves with him won't wait long. I learned how it is when I was a captive with them. Any brave can be a war chief if he can talk a bunch into following him. But he won't last long if he don't get results. Injuns don't much cotton to taking orders, anyhow." He paused. "One thing sure, they ain't going to lay hid in that brush too long, or try sniping. It ain't their way. A Comanche fights from horseback."

"They try to ride a circle, they'll be spread pretty thin."

"Yeah."

Piavah didn't ride a circle. He showed he had already laid his plan when he'd placed his braves. For suddenly a bugle sounded discordantly, no particular call, and the braves leaped onto horses and raced yelling, their paths like the converging spokes of a wheel, toward the town.

"Wonder where he got that bugle," Lynch said.

"One way or another, from an Army trumpeter."

At four hundred yards the Comanches who had rifles began firing. Others unlimbered bows and fitted arrows, no mean trick on the back of a racing pony.

Then abruptly spurts of smoke came from hiding spots among the store buildings, and here and there a Comanche or his pony went down.

"Well, they were ready for them, anyway," Kelso said.

Lynch said, "I'm going in." He swung up into his saddle, still holding the lead rope of his spare animal.

"What for?"

"I got a reason."

"You're a damn fool," Kelso said. "We'd be more help maybe sniping at them from behind."

"How long you think we'd last?"

"How long you think you'll last on a run into town?"

Lynch shrugged. "I'm going. You suit yourself."

"You must have a big reason."

"I have," Lynch said, and kicked his heels into his mount.

Kelso swore, even as he hauled aboard his own. Lynch was racing fast and thirty yards ahead of him as he fell in behind.

The Comanches were so intent on their attack that Lynch pulled into their converging midst before he was noticed, and Kelso was on his heels.

In the thick swirl of dust the Comanches did not immediately notice them as whites, and they thundered through and into the town along with the raiders. The Comanches swept up the main street, firing wildly with guns and arrows, shouting war cries and yelping. There was a lot of missing on both sides, and then the attackers were gone back into the brush.

Kelso and Lynch reined up in the middle of the street, and bullets sang around them as they sat screened by dust and shouting at the townsfolk to cease fire.

Kelso felt hot lead nip at the side of his leg above his boot top and yelled, "Stop, you frigging bastards!"

Lynch yelled, too, and the whites stopped shooting and peered at them through the settling dust.

Kelso caught sight of a chubby figure wear-

ing a smock and holding a pistol, and recognized him as Rademacher, the barber, and
shouted, "Hold your fire dammit!"

Chapter 7

Rademacher recognized Kelso and lowered his gun and said, "You're the ranger who brought Sam Lynch through last year." His eyes flicked to the side and saw Lynch, and his expression changed.

Kelso thought he saw surprise, then fear and anger in the barber's face.

"Are you crazy?" Rademacher said to Lynch. "To come back here again — ain't you already done enough?"

Lynch said, "I rode in to help."

"Help? Help? Why, you crazy sonofabitch, you're the reason those Comanches are out there now getting ready to wipe us all out."

Kelso said, "They got here first."

"Are you as stupid as he is?" Rademacher said. "He's got every rancher and townsman in this part of Texas sweating. We all've heard what this bastard done up on the reservation, killing Kwahadies there. Scalping them, by God! And alive, so they know who done it. We been sweating for a month and now it's happened. This crazy sonofabitch has roused them Comanches till they're ready to annihilate every settler in the Panhandle."

Lynch said, "Look what they done to me."

Murdock appeared in the doorway of his store and came rapidly toward them carrying a rifle, and a half-dozen other men, most in ranch clothes, came from other scattered positions.

Rademacher said, "To you. What did they do, except lift your hair. You're alive, ain't you? Which is a hell of a lot more than a lot of settlers are going to be before this is over."

Murdock reached them in time to hear Rademacher's words. He glanced in surprise at Kelso and Lynch, and his eyes fastened on the latter. He said, "Sam, what he says is the truth. What you've done is touch a match to northwest Texas. Maybe you didn't know what you was doing. But you know now — just look out there at them Comanch getting ready to make another charge."

"How many men are in town?" Kelso said. "Enough to beat them off?"

Murdock shrugged. "We're some lucky. It's Saturday and we got ranchers in for weekly trading. Lucky them bastards out there don't carry a calendar with them."

"That's Piavah in the lead."

"Worse luck," Murdock said. "He's damn

near as crazy as Lynch here. Two of a kind. Nobody knows what either of them is liable to do."

"I had a reason for what I done," Lynch said. He jerked off his hat to expose his scarred skull.

"Put your hat back on," Murdock said. "I saw what your head looked like when you came back here two months ago to see Annie."

Somebody yelled from near the saloon, "Here they come again!"

Murdock said, "You men get back to your positions."

The others moved back fast to where they had been. A few hundred yards out in all directions the war cries of the Comanches sounded. The townsmen could hear the pounding hoofs racing in toward them again, and they opened fire and the Indians did, too, and amid the staccato blasts they could hear the sharp cries as here and there a bullet found its target.

Kelso said, "Good thing it's Saturday, all right."

Murdock grunted. "Been yesterday, we'd had less than twenty men, and them mostly shopkeepers like me. Hell, ain't many of us could hit an Injun at more than six feet, less'n it's by pure luck. Them ranchers is saving the day."

It appeared so, as Piavah's men spun around and rode off again. Murdock said, "You've fought Injuns before. How long you figure they'll keep this up?"

Kelso shrugged. He reloaded his rifle and looked over at Lynch and said, "Didn't know you'd already revisited the town here."

When Lynch said nothing, Rademacher said, "He come back to see Annie."

"Shut up!" Lynch said.

Rademacher gave him a cold glance but dropped the issue. He said to nobody in particular, "That's twice we beat them off. How many times you think we can do that?"

Kelso said, "I saw the Injuns pick up two of theirs off the ground and sling them between their horses the way they do. Could be dead or only wounded. We got any hit?"

"Couple of flesh wounds, far as I know. We just been lucky. I reckon it'll get worse instead of better."

Lynch said, "They won't keep charging the same way. They tried to override us and they been beat off. They'll be trying something new."

"What?" Murdock asked.

Lynch didn't answer. Then he said, "Here they come." He was lying prone, his rifle propped by his elbows. He fired.

As if this was a signal, the Comanches suddenly swerved and spread and began riding the traditional circle a hundred yards out around the town. They fired their weapons as they rode, aiming badly. There was the sound of glass shattering as wild bullets struck a window here and there. A few bucks slung themselves low behind their horses and shot arrows from beneath the animals' necks. The arrows fell short. The bullets did not. They were mostly showing off.

Rademacher yelped and slapped his hand over the side of his neck, and when Kelso looked at him he could see blood oozing from between the barber's fingers.

Rademacher pulled his hand away and looked at the blood on it and began to swear at Lynch. "Two inches over and you'd have murdered me, you bastard."

Lynch turned to face him and said, "What you talking about?"

"You. You brought all this onto us. You think them Comanches would be here shooting at us if you hadn't riled them up the way you done?"

"I had good cause," Lynch said stubbornly.

"Good cause! You think you had good cause enough to get us all killed on account of you?"

Lynch said, "How did I know this would happen?"

"Did you ever think about it?" Rademacher

78

said. "Did you ever think of what the consequences would be?"

"I had reason for what I done," Lynch said. He took his hand from his rifle and made the reflexive gesture toward his hat.

"Keep your goddam hat on," Rademacher said. "I don't want to see your head again. Even scalped, you got more hair outside your head than you got brains inside it."

Lynch dropped his hand and pressed his trigger and shot a show-offing Comanche off his horse. His expression of resentment toward Rademacher disappeared as exultation took its place. "Got another one," he said.

"That only leaves an army of them," Rademacher said sarcastically. He turned to Kelso. "The biggest mistake I ever made," he said, "was to help you pull that arrow out of him last year."

Kelso was getting sick and tired of Rademacher's criticism of Lynch. He fired a round at a brave riding past. Then he said, his cheek still against his rifle stock, "Don't blame yourself too hard — you weren't much help."

"Now ain't that a hell of a thing to say."

"Just trying to make you feel better."

The barber mopped at the skin wound on his neck with a handkerchief, then pressed it hard against the flesh to stop the bleeding.

He scowled, but he didn't say anything more.

Murdock said, "If we beat off these Comanches, Lynch, you ride on out of here and don't ever come back."

Kelso suddenly saw a brave ride up to the circling riders, carrying a smoking torch of grease brush. A rider with a bow halted beside him and lighted an arrow from the torch and shot it high in the direction of the mercantile roof. The flaming arrow disappeared from Kelso's sight, leaving a wispy trail of smoke. Kelso shot at the brave with the torch and saw him slump, and then both braves were gone from his sight behind some out buildings. "Now they're getting smart," he said.

"My God!" Murdock said. "If that roof ignites I'll lose my store." He ran out into the street to look at it. Then he ran into the store and ran out again with a ladder. A moment later he ran back in and came out with a blanket.

Rademacher shoved his pistol into his waistband and ran over to him. Over his shoulder he said, "His place burns, my shop goes to — and the whole town with it."

Kelso and Lynch kept up a covering fire at the braves racing by. They weren't easy targets to hit, the way they kept slipping around and ducking behind their horses' necks.

Kelso said, "Shoot for the horses," and dropped a spotted stallion with his next shot. The Comanche riding it hit the ground running and caught the hand of the brave behind him, bounding up so the two could ride on together.

"Just like acrobats," Kelso said, and shot again and saw a horse go down and its rider disappear behind its carcass for protection. "Tricky bastards," he said.

"For them, it's fun," Lynch said. "Ain't none of them is afraid to die in battle. They live to die that way. I hate the sonofabitches, but I never saw a coward among them."

"Mighty peculiar folks," Kelso said. "Keep shooting. I'll take a look and see if the place is burning down." He went out onto the street and looked up.

Murdock had placed the ladder against the side of his store, but Kelso couldn't see the roof because of the building's false front. He moved to the side and could see then that Murdock and Rademacher were both perched precariously on the sloping gable, beating the opened blanket against the burning shingles, trying to smother the flames. The shingles were tinder dry, and they were having a bad time of it. Blood was running down the barber's neck and soaking his shirt, but he was only aware of the fire.

Kelso heard yelling at the end of the street and saw a man in rancher's clothes pointing at smoke rising from the roof of the saloon.

Emory, with a holstered gun and cartridge belt strapped high around his aproned belly, ran out of the saloon, stopped to look at where the rancher pointed, then moved about in a panic. The rancher reached out a hand and stopped him. The barkeep tore loose and ran to a water barrel standing on the saloon porch, but then ran back to stand beside the rancher again. The smoke abruptly stopped, and Kelso hoped the flame had gone out of its own accord, because it looked like the saloon man had no idea of what to do if it hadn't.

Kelso went back to his position beside Lynch.

"How's it look?" Lynch said.

"Store's under control. Don't know about the saloon."

Lynch straightened up. "The saloon is burning?"

"I ain't sure. It started."

"I got to get down there."

"Why?"

"That's where Annie works." Lynch started to move off.

"Nobody'd be working there now." Kelso grabbed his sleeve.

Lynch jerked loose. "You don't understand. Annie *lives* there."

"She wouldn't be there now."

"How do you know? She may be sleeping and —"

"Sleeping? With all this shooting going on?"

Lynch looked suddenly sheepish. He turned back to face the revolving Comanches, and said, "Yeah, I was forgetting."

Whatever Annie was, Kelso thought, she had a hell of a hold on Sam if she made him forget he was fighting Comanches.

They were pulling out of range again. The people in Bonner could see them far out on the prairie having a powwow.

Kelso said, "I wish I had a Sharps buffalo gun. I'd give them a surprise then."

Lynch said, "I'm going to the saloon. If it's on fire —"

"I'll go with you," Kelso said. "Those braves are going to talk it over some out there."

They went down the middle of the main street, side by side. They could see no smoke coming from the saloon roof now. The fire on the roof of Murdock's place was out, too.

The saloon owner, Emory, was still standing in front of his place as they approached. He turned as they came up. He saw Lynch, and the dazed expression on his face turned into a scowl. "You!" he said.

"Where's Annie?"

"What the hell do you care?"

"Where is she?"

"Inside," the saloon man said. "But she don't want to see you, no more than the rest of us. Maybe less."

Lynch went to the doors of the saloon and went in.

Kelso said, "He still loves that girl." He paused. "Was it her that set him off on his rampage?"

"Hell, no! It was *him* that set him off! She never was in love with him, he only thought she was. Don't try to blame Annie for what happened."

Kelso nodded. "Never figured to," he said. But hearing what Emory said gave him a great sense of relief. He couldn't have said why. He followed Lynch into the place.

Inside and behind the bar Annie was standing alone, pouring herself a drink. She looked at Lynch and said, half-sobbing, "Sam. Oh, Sam, why did you do it?"

"I think you know."

"There was no reason." She looked at Kelso then, and slowly recognition came to her. "You — you're the ranger that saved his life."

"Name of Kelso. John Kelso."

"I remember." Then, suddenly, her concern deepened. "Mr. Kelso — you being a ranger — I mean is the law after Sam? For what he did up on the reservation?"

"Now, Annie —" Lynch said. "Don't you go bothering your head about —"

"I'm asking you, Mr. Kelso. Is the law after him?"

Kelso nodded.

"You! You have a warrant for his arrest?"

"If I get a Texan jury, I'll be all right," Lynch said. "Don't you be fretting none about me."

She downed the drink she had poured. "Why did you have to start all this trouble? Is it all because I said there was never anything big between us? Why didn't you just believe me?"

"I had plenty reason," Lynch said.

Kelso said, "Let's go, Sam. Those Comanches will be acting up again pretty soon."

Gunfire sounded. A bullet smashed a rear window, came through the thin wood partition of a back room and thudded into the framework of the front wall.

"It ain't safe for you here," Lynch said.

She began to laugh hysterically. "Safe? Not safe? And whose fault is that, Sam?" She looked at Kelso and said, "How do you think I feel, knowing it's part my fault those damn renegades are out there ready to exterminate every person in the Panhandle? And all because I couldn't convince him nothing changed between us?"

"Not too good, I reckon," Kelso said. Then, to Lynch, "Sam, we got fighting to do. Those Comanches are riding circle again."

Annie went on, as if Kelso hadn't spoken. "You want to know why? He didn't *want* to believe me. He wanted to go after his revenge on those Comanches he hates so much. He wanted more reason to do that. He *wanted* to believe I rejected him, so he could keep his hate hot!"

Kelso looked again at Lynch. Lynch was keeping a poker face, but there was no sign of denial there. "That right, Sam?"

Lynch seemed to dissemble, a perplexed expression replacing his blank mask. He said, as if wondering aloud, "Might be I did, and I didn't know it then."

"And now it's too late," Annie said. "You've got everybody in this part of Texas down on you, Sam. You've got a warrant out for your arrest and trial. Right now, you're in the hands of the ranger sent to bring you in. How are you ever going to get out of this mess you've brought down on yourself?"

Lynch was silent.

Annie gave him a long, searching look, then began openly to cry.

"Come on, Sam," Kelso said again. "We got fighting to do."

Lynch trailed him out, hesitantly, looking back once over his shoulder at Annie. She caught his glance and deliberately turned away. She picked up the bottle and poured herself another drink and shuddered.

Outside, Kelso could hear the guns firing at the Comanches all around the town. But waiting in the protection of the portico were Rademacher and Murdock and Emory and a couple of other shopkeepers.

Murdock said, "Ranger, do you speak Comanche?"

"No," Kelso said. "But Lynch here does."

"That won't do," Rademacher said, "seeing as to what we figure to do concerns him personal."

"What's that?"

"We want to dicker with Piavah," Rademacher said. "We got to stop this attack before some flaming arrow starts the town on fire."

"Dicker how?"

Rademacher said, "Lynch, if you're any kind of a man, you'll give yourself up to Piavah in trade for him leaving the rest of us alone."

"Like hell," Lynch said. "He gets me, he'll skin me alive over a slow fire. I seen my share of Comanche torture, and I don't figure to ever have none of it done to me."

Emory and the other two merchants had got behind Kelso and Lynch, and one of them said, "Don't make no funny moves with them weapons. Even I ain't going to miss at four feet distance with this hand gun."

Neither Lynch nor Kelso moved.

Then a voice called from the saloon door, "One of you damn fools touch Sam and you'll get a blast from this Greener!"

They turned and saw Annie standing there, with one batwing open and the double barrel of the barkeep's sawed-off shotgun pointed at them.

"Stay out of this, Annie!" Emory said.

"Stay out, hell! You idiots stop and think what you're intending."

"We intend to trade off Lynch to save the town," Emory said.

"You think those Comanches could be trusted to pull out? Think what you're doing — to turn over a white man to be tortured and murdered and those renegades will likely burn the town anyway. You want to live with that on your conscience?"

The shopkeepers looked uneasy. Also a little scared of that shotgun. Annie was crying openly now, and who the hell knew what she might do with it.

"You want to save the town, you better keep Sam and the ranger fighting at your side," she said.

Murdock said, "Could be we acted a mite spooked." He looked at the others and none of them could meet another's eyes. "It's just them fires that spooked us, maybe."

Annie bobbed the shotgun up and down and stepped out on the porch, and they could see then that she was a little drunk, as well as maybe hysterical.

Murdock said tightly, "Now don't you go doing nothing rash, Annie."

"Don't none of *you* do anything rash," she said. "Get out there and fight those Comanches off. You're Texans, aren't you?"

"All right," Murdock said. "All right, Annie."

"Wait a minute," Emory said. "I ain't so sure."

But the others were moving off and they left him there standing alone. He looked at Annie and met her eyes over the shotgun.

She said, "Damn you, Emory!" Then she turned and went back into the saloon.

"Well, hell," Emory said. "You can't argue with a woman."

Two things happened abruptly.

The Comanches pulled away from the town and fled to the south.

And from the north, a swirling of dust appeared and a patrol of a dozen black troopers of the Tenth Cavalry rode in, led by a white lieutenant.

"We heard the firing," the lieutenant said to Kelso. "We pushed hard to get here."

Kelso could see by their sweating mounts that this was so. It was another time the cavalry had arrived where needed, and by pure luck, as was almost the only way it ever happened, he thought. He remembered the colonel at Fort Sill telling him the Tenth was in the field somewhere in the area — and thank God for that!

The lieutenant was seasoned and cynical. He listened as Kelso briefed him on the Comanche attack. Then he said, "We'll not pursue them. Not now. We'd only kill off the horses." He eyed Kelso speculatively. "Word was out the rangers were given the job of hunting down Sam Lynch."

"Yeah," Kelso said. "Ever see him?"

The lieutenant shook his head. "You the one they sent to do it?"

"Matter of fact, I am." At that moment Lynch came up to join them.

"I understand they butchered up his head

real bad when they scalped him," the lieutenant said.

"They did that," Kelso said. He was hoping there was nothing about Lynch to rouse the officer's suspicions, although he wasn't sure just why this was.

The lieutenant studied Lynch. "Don't often see one of those *californio* hats around here," he said.

Lynch said easily, "Yeah. But me, I always been partial to them."

"Well," the lieutenant said, "good luck catching that crazy bastard. I hear he's like a Comanche himself. I hope you get him before he stirs up any more trouble on the frontier. The Army doesn't need any more of that. Especially not with Comanches. Only way Colonel Ranald Mackenzie whipped them a few years back was because he surprised half the Comanche nation asleep in their Palo Duro hideout, mostly by luck."

Kelso said, "Meaning no offense, Lieutenant, but Mackenzie was one of a kind. Even though he was a Yankee officer, me and most Texans respect him as the greatest Injun fighter the Army ever had."

"I think I'd agree with you on that," the lieutenant said. He turned at the sound of a commotion behind him.

Emory came running up the street, hollering.

"Now, what the hell?" Kelso said.

"They took Annie!" Emory yelled. "The Comanches took Annie!"

Chapter 8

"One of them red bastards must have got into the back of the saloon and carried her off," Emory said. "Must have done it while we had our eyes on these soldiers coming up."

"How you know it was an Injun?"

"You know Annie. She must have put up a hell of a fight. Ripped the breechclout right off some buck. It's laying there along with a feather she must have snatched out of his headband. There's a lot of blood on the floor, like maybe he hurt her."

Rademacher was there now, and he said, "Knowing Annie, maybe she broke the Injun's nose."

Emory said, "What's important is there's a naked Comanche out there now riding off with my saloon's star attraction."

Lynch was already heading for his horses.

Kelso said to the lieutenant, "You coming?"

The officer hesitated, then shook his head. "Like I said, our mounts are beat. No way we could catch them."

"Wish me luck then."

"You're going after them alone?"

"Not alone. The two of us."

"What did you say your friend's name was?"

"I didn't say," Kelso said. "But that's a white woman they took." He was in a sweat that Rademacher would identify Lynch, but he didn't.

The officer frowned. Then he said, "I'm not Mackenzie. And I don't have spare horses like he had. How far could I get?"

"So be it," Kelso said.

"We'll track you tomorrow, just in case."

"Yeah," Kelso said. "You do that, Lieutenant." He turned abruptly and walked fast in the direction Lynch had gone.

As he came up, Lynch drew his handgun. "I'm going after her, you understand? That's my woman them bastards took."

Kelso nodded. "Put it away. Our truce still holds — until we get her back."

Lynch holstered his gun, and they mounted and rode south out of town, leading the spare horses. Lynch said, "Glad you see it this way. One of us was going to die back there if you didn't."

"I knew that. But it didn't influence my thinking."

"Reckon you taken a liking to Annie, then?"

"She's a woman, ain't she?"

"That she is," Lynch said. "And I get her back, she's going to feel about me like she used to."

Kelso didn't have the heart to remind him that he was under arrest.

Now they settled down to following the broad tracks left by the band of Comanches. The country here was prairie. The Indians were moving fast along the old Comanche Trail toward Mexico. Kelso wondered if they could ever catch them at a spot to attempt a rescue before they reached the harsh country of the Big Bend region. Or even there.

Kelso had been through part of it once, a few years back, with a handful of other rangers. They'd been hot on the trail of a Chiso Apache marauder who made the area the home of his band. At that time the Apaches had given them the slip. He hoped now that his and Lynch's efforts would not be as futile.

The Chiso Apaches were really a band of the Mescalero tribe. They preyed on the Mexicans of Chihuahua, too, as well as Texans. But they disappeared whenever a Comanche raiding party moved through their stomping grounds. The Apaches had learned many years ago to avoid fighting the Comanches if it was at all possible.

Which gave you an idea, Kelso thought, of how fiercely savage the Comanches were. They scared even the Apaches, and the Apaches were afraid of nothing else.

The Big Bend region was the roughest in Texas, and Kelso figured they would have to make their try there if they were ever going to rescue Annie.

The thought came to him then that his original job of bringing in Lynch was being considerably complicated by the girl. But, hell, he would never turn his back on *any* woman captured by the Indians. It was the way he was built. And with Annie — well, he had to face it, he'd been attracted to her from the first, from that time last year when he had first seen her in Bonner.

There was a time element here, too. For a true Moon Raid, Piavah had to conduct it during the full of the September harvest moon. This was the ritualistic way of the old Comanches, the way it had been since early times. If Piavah wanted to follow the tradition, he wouldn't waste any more time on the trail.

So, if Kelso and Lynch were going to make a try for Annie, it would have to be in the Bend, before Piavah got into Mexico.

* ★ *

They crossed the Pecos, and the Comanches
held their lead. And then came the time when
they could see the peaks of the Santiagos, and
knew that there somewhere was a gap through
which went the old war trail. And now the
far, faint rising of the Comanches' dust could
no longer be seen.

Lynch said tightly, "We're losing them."

"No," Kelso said. "They just went through
the pass."

On either side of them the sparse grassland
faded into shimmering flats of brush and cactus. Above them the sky was made of brass.

They began to wonder whether they would
be able to find water. They had only a little
left in their canteens, and in the September
heat it would not last long.

There was always a possibility of rain in
this season, but hours later, when they found
the gap and reached its summit and looked
out on the deep-slashed maze of canyons that
lay ahead, they were fearful of a rain even
while they wished for it. It would take only
a short time to turn those dry barrancas into
flash-flood channels that could destroy them.

There were more than canyons in sight,
though. There were cactus-filled flats, too,
and hills of sand and rock and bare talus. It
was a devil's mix of mountains and mesas,

arroyos and gorges, a landscape of harsh beauty. And off on the south horizon loomed the purplish saw-toothed peaks of the Chisos. Kelso understood then why *sierra,* the Spanish word for saw, meant mountain range as well.

They were lucky and found a spring on the south slope of the summit. They watered the horses and refilled their canteens and made camp there as sunset brought a wild confusion of blues and reds and purples to the country. And then, abruptly, darkness flowed in to fill the crevices, making islands of the distant peaks; and then they, too, were submerged. The air grew cold, but they were afraid to light a fire that might attract the Comanches.

They got up at first light, stiff and surly and not speaking. They saddled spare mounts and descended into the maze.

A long time later, Lynch spoke first. As if he had been thinking about it for a long while, he said, "If I get her free, it'll be like it used to be between us. Annie and me, I mean."

Kelso shook his head, but said nothing. One thing about Sam Lynch, he thought, he had a one-track mind.

The trail led them in an easy climb to another, lower pass, flanked by escarpments. Kelso halted just before they topped out, and dismounted. "Best have a look."

Lynch got down too, and they approached the rim cautiously. Kelso went prone, and peered into a long, narrow valley. A purplish haze hung over it, but visibility was good enough that he could see a thin floating of dust at the far end. He studied it for a long time, and it seemed to him that the dust disappeared into a canyon beyond.

He said, "You see it?"

"Yeah. Could be them."

"I figured they'd be further ahead. Strange, ain't it?"

"Yeah. Looks like something slowed them up," Lynch said. "Well, you can't ever tell about an Injun."

They went back to the horses and mounted and began the ride down toward the valley.

And now, because they were sure that Piavah's bunch had entered the far canyon, they rode relaxed, Kelso's mind searching for some plan of action that might free the girl from her captors.

His thoughts were shattered by the glint of sunlight striking metal fifty yards up the escarpment to his right.

"Don't look," he said to Lynch. "But there's a rifle pointed at us from that west scarp."

"What we going to do about it?"

"There's some cover in those rocks up

ahead. Keep riding like we don't know he's there. Unless he shoots."

"And if he does?"

"Go for the rocks — fast."

They rode at their steady pace. Lynch said, "Goddam it! That's twice you walked into a trap. Last time was when that curly-headed breed Comanche took you up near Bonner."

"I may be getting too old for this business," Kelso said. "What's your excuse?"

Lynch rode a few yards, then said grudgingly, "I reckon it could happen to anybody." Then, "Wonder why he don't shoot?"

"Strange, all right. Maybe he don't want to set us running."

They reached the rocks and were hid from the escarpment.

That's when a guttural voice called out in strangely accented Spanish, "Drop the *pistolas!*"

What Lynch had just jibed him about, walking into another trap, was still rankling Kelso. He was suddenly recklessly stubborn. "No, by God!" he said. "You show your face first."

"*Mira las rocas,*" the voice said.

Kelso looked at the rocks around him. Eight or ten weapon barrels were shoved into sight, all pointing at him. Behind the weapons he glimpsed shoulder-length black hair and Indian faces.

Lynch saw them too, and went into action. He rammed his spurs into his horse and went racing down into the valley.

He took the ambushers by surprise, and they scrambled around in the rocks to get a bead on him. He was a hundred yards away before they got off the first shot, and then he was plunging into a screening of brush and was out of sight. But not before a bullet dropped the extra horse he was leading.

Kelso flicked his glance to the Indians, wondering why they didn't run for their own mounts which had ought to be hid close by.

Instead, one of them stepped from cover, holding a revolver, an old Remington Army .44. He called out something Kelso couldn't understand to the other bucks, and they came out into the open. Kelso recognized his voice as the one who had called out to him.

He was obviously the leader, and he was not young. He was short like most Comanches, but not of their usual blocky build. He had a wide, thin, straight slash of a mouth.

Kelso met his eyes, doubt in his mind. He said, in Spanish, "You are not Piavah?"

The Indian said, "You are trailing the Comanches?"

Kelso saw no use in denying it. He nodded. He was bothered by uncertainty. There was something here not clear to him.

The leader said, "We are Apache."

Kelso kicked himself for not recognizing the fact. But it had been four years since he'd been in a patrol against them. And he'd always had some of the typical white man's inability to distinguish easily between the tribes.

The Apache chief said, "The white-eyes and the Mexicans call me Algaday." He watched Kelso's face and smiled faintly at the startled expression which flitted there.

"Algaday!" Kelso said.

"You know the name, eh? You were with a force of rangers who tried to hunt me down, it makes many seasons now. I recognize you."

"You were that close?" Kelso said.

"At one time I was only twenty paces from you."

Kelso said, "We did not catch sight of you that time."

Algaday regarded him with amusement. "You are honest, ranger. You had the luck that I had only one cartridge in my gun and there were many of you. To fire it at you would have been a foolish thing. You, all of you rangers, rode right on by."

"It is a difficult thing to catch an Apache," Kelso said.

"Yet, you try to catch a Comanche."

"The Comanches are the enemies of the Apaches, is it not true?" Kelso said.

Algaday nodded. "And that is why we do not chase your friend. You had better get down from your saddle."

Kelso dismounted. One of the Apaches came and led away his horse.

Algaday said, "Those Comanches, they stole our horses last night."

"They are good horse stealers," Kelso said.

Algaday said, "There is nothing an Apache hates worse than a Comanche. As far back as any Apache can remember, or his father's father before him, the Comanches have made war on us.

"Why do you tell me this?"

"You have a horse and a gun and are a fighting man. And I would rather have you on my side against the Comanche horse stealers."

"You are proposing friendship?"

A faint smile played on Algaday's thin lips. "I propose a temporary peace between us. Against a common enemy."

"It appears I have no choice."

"Very true," Algaday said.

"And my partner?"

"The same for him — if we find him."

Kelso said, "You want to recover your horses. We want to recover a woman the Comanches have taken from us."

"You would risk your life for a woman?"

103

"You risk yours for horses."

"Horses have value."

Kelso nodded. "To Piavah's Comanches, obviously."

"*Piavah*," Algaday repeated. "I will remember that name." Then he said, "Your partner, he will try to free you from us?"

Kelso shrugged. "I don't know. He mostly wants to get the woman back."

"The woman is his, then?"

Kelso thought about this, then nodded.

"He is a warrior?"

"He has killed and scalped Comanches."

A surprised interest showed on Algaday's face. "This is true? Then I would welcome him with us."

Kelso thought, I hope to hell Lynch doesn't try anything rash now. Not when we've got a dozen Apaches on our side. Just like the ill-starred bastard to attack them and ruin everything.

He said, "We best be on our way. The Comanches are heading for a raid in Mexico."

Algaday grunted. "I will ride your horse."

"I call myself Kelso," Kelso said.

Algaday nodded. "*Kelso*," he said. "All right, Kelso. You will walk."

"You think you can overtake Piavah, walking?"

"We Apaches can, running."

"I heard you could run seventy miles in a day," Kelso said. "It is unfortunate that I cannot."

Algaday frowned, then shrugged. "You ride, then. But do not try to escape."

"I will not try." Kelso began to see the possibility of rescuing the woman. That's if Lynch didn't do something crazy and spoil it all.

Algaday motioned for a couple of his braves to pick up Kelso's weapons. "These, we will keep until we catch the Comanches," he said. "You understand?"

"I understand," Kelso said.

Chapter 9

The Apaches set off on foot and Kelso trotted his horse to match them. They just might overtake Piavah's bunch at that, he thought, if Piavah didn't push too hard. A lot depended on whether Piavah knew the Apaches were following him. Kelso hoped the Apaches didn't trot him into a Comanche ambush. This sudden Apache encounter had been enough to shorten his life by a couple of years; he wasn't ready for another jolt like that just yet.

Algaday jogged along beside Kelso's horse. The Apache chief had to have ten or fifteen years up on Kelso, and yet he had enough wind to carry on a conversation while he ran. It was hard to believe.

Now Algaday said, "It has been many seasons since the Comanches last came down their trail into Mexico."

"The white chief Mackenzie drove them onto a reservation," Kelso said.

"I heard something of this," Algaday said. "But I did not believe it. The Comanches driven onto a reservation! This one called Mackenzie must be a great war chief of the whites."

"Perhaps the greatest."

"They used to come down every season of the long moon. But only to pass through. For us Mescaleros of the Chiso band these mountains have been our home for three generations. That will be our advantage — we know the land much better than the Comanches."

"I hope that is true."

"You will see," Algaday said. "The Comanche is fierce like the wolf, but the Apache is sly like the coyote."

"I hope that is true, also." Then Kelso said, "You speak well in Spanish. How is it that you have learned?"

"I long had a Mexican wife. We, too, have often raided in Mexico."

"Of course," Kelso said. "I was forgetting."

"And in Texas."

"That I was not forgetting."

Algaday grinned broadly at that. He seemed to take it as a compliment. Then he said, "How is it that this Piavah is not on the reservation, then?"

"He left to hunt my partner. My partner had killed some of his braves on the reservation — a matter of vengeance."

"Vengeance for what?"

"For being scalped alive the year before."

"He attacked the Comanches single-handed on the reservation?"

"He took four scalps there."

"I hope he will join us."

"If we find him, and I can talk to him," Kelso said, "he will."

"Only the Comanches would have stolen our horses on the way to a raid. They cannot help themselves. There is no people as *loco* for horses."

"It would be hard to catch them if they reach Mexico."

"*Sí*," Algaday said. "And we must fight them before they reach San Carlos."

"San Carlos?"

"A little town just below the border. It is a truce town, even for warring tribes. Many years ago, certain tribes who were pressed by their enemies promised to be good friends with the Mexicans there if they were given sanctuary. Other tribes, fleeing from pony soldiers or you rangers, made the same agreement. Now you will find sworn enemies living on the outskirts of San Carlos side by side. It has become a place of temporary refuge and trade. Sometimes you will find Comanches, Apaches, Kiowas, Lipans, even Kickapoos and Tonkawas there — gringo outlaws too. So we must hit the Comanches before they reach San Carlos."

Kelso said, "You would not fight there?"

"To fight there," Algaday said, "would destroy our sanctuary. It is a safe place where we can trade for guns and bullets, a place where we can sell what we rob from other Chihuahua towns or from Texas. A place of business for all. It would not do to destroy it. Also, for that reason, we never harm or steal from a Mexican of San Carlos."

"A cozy arrangement," Kelso said. "Something like the Comancheros of Santa Fe had with the Comanches of the Staked Plains."

"Exactly," Algaday said. "Everybody profits from the arrangement."

"Except those who are raided."

Algaday shrugged and trotted on, suddenly silent.

They passed through the narrow valley and into an arid basin of catclaw, agave, mesquite and Spanish bayonet. The trail was obvious enough, the horses of the Comanches had renewed the old war trail.

"We are in plain sight if Piavah looks back," Kelso said.

Algaday shook his head. "He is moving fast and is into the barrancas by now. There is where we will hope to fight him."

"Barrancas?"

"There are hundreds of them — all known to us Apaches."

"And the Comanches?"

"They know only the main trail."

"How can you catch up with them?"

"They will camp tonight. We will not," Algaday said. "They will not remember how far an Apache can run. Therefore, they will not expect us."

Kelso said, "I would never have believed a man could outrun a horse."

"Only an Apache can. A Comanche cannot run at all. He lives too much on his horse."

"Do you see the tracks of Lynch?"

Algaday shook his head. "They are lost among the rest." He trotted silently, breathing easily. Then he said, "If he is following."

"He is following them," Kelso said. "I told you that they have his woman." He was wondering how Lynch could hope to rescue her, alone. The crazy bastard would try, he supposed. How had he waylaid those Kwahadies he'd killed on the reservation? The man was like an Indian himself, Kelso thought, a lot of Comanche had rubbed off on him during his years of captivity.

Kelso said now to Algaday, "The rough country begins up ahead?"

"The roughest," the Apache said. "The Apaches have a legend that when the Great Spirit, Yosen, finished making the world, he had many rocks left over. And he threw them into one pile. And there is where he threw them."

"Then Lynch will try to rescue the woman there."

They were nearing the vast, wild, jumbled rock country now, and the Apaches dropped back to a walk. Algaday said, "You will go the rest of the way on foot — with us."

"And my horse?"

"We will let one of our *viejos,* our old one, hold him and follow a distance behind. We will take no chances on the horse signaling the Comanche horses. We must depend on surprise."

Kelso got down from his saddle, and Algaday motioned to an old Apache who, though toothless, was even now catching up to them with a laborious trot.

"An old man, to still be running," Kelso said.

Algaday gave his faint, thin smile. "Would you believe he has more than seventy years? And he will not like to be chosen to stay back holding the horse." He turned to the *viejo* and spoke in the clicking, guttural tongue of the Apaches.

The old man scowled fiercely and talked back at Algaday, who listened unruffled until the old man ran down, then uttered what sounded to be a repetition of his order. The old man took on a sullen look, but he grabbed the trailing reins of the horse and stood waiting until the rest had moved out a considerable ways ahead. Then he swung onto the mount and followed at a slow walk.

It was late afternoon now. The sun had gone behind a towering ridge to the west, and shadows were already filling the labyrinth of barrancas cut deep into the mix of sedimentary limestone and igneous volcanic rock.

Kelso could easily understand the old Apache legend of the country's formation.

And then suddenly Algaday halted and raised his hand. There was the smell of smoke in the air. Up ahead, the Comanches had made an early camp.

Algaday, with Kelso beside him, crept close through a cover of hackberry and piñon, and there they were in a bend of stream bed, now dry, camped on a wide expanse of gravelly sand. Off to one side was a thick stand of the sad-looking weeping juniper.

And tied to the trunk of one of these was a sadder sight: Sam Lynch stripped completely naked.

In a semicircle around him, squatting and standing braves watched expectantly. Piavah himself stood near Lynch, and as Kelso watched he reached out and grabbed Lynch by an ear and jerked his head forward, then slammed it back against the juniper trunk with a force that caused a sound like a dropped melon. Some of the watching braves laughed, and Kelso swore under his breath.

It was clear now why they had made early camp. They had somehow got their hands on Lynch and were taking time to have their fun with him.

Kelso swept the audience with his eyes and was not surprised when he saw Annie huddled between two stocky Comanches. She looked white and shaken, and although he viewed her from the side and sixty yards away, he thought she was biting her lip to keep from crying out. Her saloon dress was torn and filthy from trail dust, and the exposed parts of her body were smudged or bruised or both.

Now Piavah took a knife from his belt and held the point of it against Lynch's bared genitals. Lynch tried to twist from the touch but was bound fast by a rope around his thighs which held him tight to the tree.

The Comanches laughed, high-pitched and wild with anticipation. But Piavah wasn't ready yet. This was only a teaser to make Lynch squirm, to fill him with terror. He withdrew the knife and picked up a sharpened splinter, pinched the flesh on Lynch's belly and rammed the splinter through and left it there. Lynch's face turned the color of ashes.

Algaday tapped Kelso's shoulder and gestured for him to withdraw. When he felt they were out of hearing of the Comanches, Algaday said, "Your friend has been a fool."

"With your help we can save him," Kelso said. "And the woman."

Algaday said, "Our intent is to regain our horses. It will be a distraction when it is discovered they are taken. That is the help we give you. A chance for you to rescue your friends."

"Only that?"

"It is enough," the Apache said. "It is clear to me how it could be done."

"You will not help me fight them?"

"I do not like to fight Comanches," Algaday said. "That will be up to you."

Kelso said bitterly, "You think, of course, that I may be the one providing the distraction — for you."

Algaday grinned. "I told you the Apache is like the coyote. Never forget, either, that the Apache hates the white man — and, in particular, the Texas Rangers."

"If I fight alone," Kelso said, "I will not last long enough to distract them. Give me a few of your braves while you take the rest for the horses."

Algaday thought about this.

Back in the Comanche camp Kelso heard Lynch scream.

114

"Goddammit! what's your answer?" Kelso asked.

Algaday finally gave a reluctant nod. "Six, only," he said.

Kelso was waiting. With him were six of the Apaches. Algaday had taken the rest and gone for the horses. It had been agreed that once the horses were taken and started on their way, Algaday would fire a signaling shot that would draw the Comanches and give Kelso his chance to free Lynch and grab the girl.

Hidden there in the bushes, it seemed to Kelso that Algaday was taking a hell of a long time.

Now, as the minutes passed and there was no sound from Algaday, an angry doubt began to take hold of Kelso. The doubt quickly became a conviction when Kelso became suddenly aware that the Apaches who had been beside him in the brush were now gone.

He cursed himself for ever having trusted the Apache chief. He should have known better. Hadn't the double-crossing bastard told him he hated whites, especially rangers?

The situation was now clear to him. Algaday would wait until Kelso was forced to make the first move, and then take advantage of the diversion. The Apache would get away with the horses without effort then, most likely.

115

He damned sure wasn't going to fire that warning shot he'd promised.

Right now, it could be a question of who could outwait the other, Kelso or Algaday. And then he heard Lynch scream again.

He immediately began to crawl toward the sound until he had the Comanche camp again in full view. Piavah was holding his knife again and the braves were waiting expectantly. It looked to Kelso as if they were all there, including three or four who were crudely bandaged, survivors of their attack on Bonner. Even the horse guard had come in, he supposed. Nobody wanted to miss the fun. Which made it even easier for Algaday.

From where he now lay he could clearly see Annie's face. It registered complete shock, expressionlessness even, as Piavah made a swift slash across Lynch's abdomen, a deft, shallow grazing that caused a thin curtain of blood to descend toward Lynch's loins. Lynch strained against his bonds, and there were delighted chuckles from the audience.

Sweat broke out all over Kelso. Damn that goddam Apache, Algaday! If he would only fire that shot! Kelso knew now that he wouldn't. And Kelso knew he couldn't wait.

Piavah lifted his knife and slashed at Lynch's left ear lobe.

Annie shrieked.

A Comanche beside her swung his fist and knocked her over. She sprawled out full length, and the brave went to his knees and rammed his hand up under her dress and grabbed her thigh. Everybody laughed again.

Piavah called something and the brave desisted and turned back to watch the chief. Piavah touched the point of his knife to the flesh just above Lynch's right eye, and with the fingertips of his other hand, he grasped the eyelashes and pulled the lid extended.

Kelso jerked his sixgun from his holster as Piavah's blade hand moved toward Lynch's eyelid. He fired a quick shot at Piavah and it missed.

But it stopped Piavah. The Comanche chief yelled and the others sprang up and ran from the sand bar into the bushes as Kelso got off two more shots at Piavah, one of them drawing a quick spurt of blood from Piavah's shoulder. But Piavah kept running and dove into cover.

Kelso held up firing at the last fleeing brave, who was dragging Annie with him into concealment. He was afraid to shoot at this one, afraid of hitting Annie.

And then the area was cleared except for Lynch, tied to the weeping juniper, his head erect and staring toward where Kelso was hidden. Blood was dripping from his mutilated ear.

There he was. Only now he was bait for

Kelso, bait left by the Comanches who were waiting in the bushes for Kelso to make his move to free the captive.

The odds weren't exactly in Kelso's favor. And even as he hesitated, Kelso saw Lynch suddenly slump in his bonds, made weak from the agony he had undergone and from being tied there standing for God knew how long.

It was now or never, Kelso thought, and drew his hunting knife. He knew he didn't stand a chance, but he had to try.

He crouched to make his sprint and drew a deep breath.

And just then he heard Algaday's shot from where he was stealing back the horses, and the sound of hoofs striking rocky terrain on a dead run away from the place. A long Apache yell of defiance followed, and almost at once he heard the infuriated answering cries of the Comanches as they rushed after them.

Kelso reached the tree and made quick slashes at the bonds which held Lynch. As Lynch came free he collapsed to his knees, and Kelso bent quick to catch him, and that saved him as a rifle cracked in the brush and its bullet smacked into the tree trunk.

At least one Comanche had stayed behind. Kelso snapped off a shot blindly into the bushes where he thought the shot had come from.

Lynch struggled to his feet and then they were both running to get out of the clearing. Bullets kicked up gravel as the concealed rifle blasted again. Kelso felt the tug of a slug as it ripped through his pants. He caught a glimpse of a smoke puff and fired off another shot and heard the scream of a brave hard hit and writhing. And then they were in the cover.

Kelso listened for more sound from the brave he had hit. Lynch seemed not right and said in a loud voice, "Thanks," and Kelso reached out a hand and clamped it over Lynch's mouth. He did not move for a long moment; then, as he heard no movement or sound, he removed his hand and whispered. "I plugged the one that was shooting. Maybe we can get his rifle."

"We got to get Annie," Lynch said.

"We will."

"What set them Comanch to running off?"

In a few words Kelso explained about the Apaches. Then he said, "Wait here. I'm going to get that rifle." He moved cautiously toward where he'd heard the brave scream. The brave was dead, shot through the breastbone. Kelso grabbed up the rifle and a belt of cartridges the Comanche had slung Mexican style over his shoulder.

He made his way back to Lynch, and Lynch

said, "Hell, that's my own rifle and belt."

"You're in luck. Here, put the belt on."

Lynch took it and started to wrap it around his waist.

Kelso stared at him, waiting for his reaction. When it came, he burst out laughing. He said, "Missing something?"

"Hell," Lynch said, "I ain't wearing no clothes."

Kelso said, "Reckon we're both a mite shook up, not to notice."

"They stripped me just before they trussed me to that tree."

"Go get your duds. I'll cover you. Only that one brave stayed behind, I reckon."

"Let's hope none of them bastards is coming back from chasing Apaches," Lynch said. He took off running toward the tree, grunting at the pain of stepping barefoot over the sharp ground.

Kelso crouched ready with Lynch's rifle, not positive there weren't maybe a few more Comanches close by. He swore as Lynch sat down and took the time to pull his socks and boots on before he ran back naked with his clothes in his arms.

"Glad you didn't take the time to finish dressing," Kelso said, ironically.

"You ever try running barefooted over a strew of busted bottles?" Lynch said. He was pulling his pants on now and having a hard time getting the legs over his boots.

Finally, he was fully dressed except for his hat, which was missing. He said, "The goddam bastards took my hat first thing. They're right proud, it seems, of what they done to my head."

"Well, we ain't going to waste time looking for it. I ain't risking my own hair to find your hat. Let's go." Kelso started off in the direction the Indians had gone.

Lynch fell in behind, holding a handkerchief against his bleeding ear. The blood from the cut across his belly had slowly stained through his shirt, but now it was starting to clot.

They went only a few yards before Kelso stopped abruptly and Lynch smashed into him. "What the hell!"

Ahead of them was the old Apache who had been left as horse-holder of Kelso's mount, which was still held by the reins in the *viejo*'s hands. The old one was seated, leaning his wizened back against a thrust of limestone.

The horse was acting strangely, and as Kelso and Lynch came up it shied, and the old Apache fell over on his side and the horse spooked some more and took a few steps and the old Apache went dragging after.

Kelso moved up on the horse, speaking softly, and the horse eyed him wildly.

Behind him Lynch said, "Why don't he let go?"

"Can't," Kelso said. "He's got a death grip on a loop in the reins. That old Apache is dead."

"Dead?"

Kelso got close and grabbed the reins above where the Apache held them and looked down on him. He said, "He was seventy some years old, Algaday told me. And he ran a lot of miles today keeping up with them younger bucks. I reckon his heart just stopped."

"Well, we got us a horse."

"Now all we need is a plan," Kelso said. "The idea was to grab the girl when the Apaches struck for the horses. I was hoping you were still free to help."

Lynch frowned. "I went off half-cocked when I saw a bunch of them bucks about to gang her. I couldn't stand to see that and not try to save her."

"Yeah," Kelso said. "I understand." And he did. He damn sure would have done the same thing himself, the way he had come to feel about her. His feeling surprised him. Hell, he had only seen and talked to her twice, briefly. How could she take such a hold on him?

Lynch said, "Maybe you do understand. But to me, she ain't just *any* white woman.

122

She's *my* woman. I ain't give up hope yet. I wanted to marry her ever since the first time I saw her in Bonner. I didn't care that she danced and sang in a saloon. I'd have made her forget all that." He paused. "Did you know she was raised as a rancher's daughter? Run off when she was too young to know better. But she knows ranch life."

Kelso swung up on the horse and said, "Climb up behind."

"What we going to do?"

"Don't rightly know yet. But we can't let them Comanches get too far ahead. Could be the Apaches didn't get all the horses, all together there were a lot of them. Hell, they'd be tyring to drive off maybe a hundred head. Not easy under the circumstances."

"Then the Comanches will be riding again," Lynch said.

"That's what I'm thinking. Let's go."

They pushed along, yet riding cautiously, fearful of overtaking stragglers and of fatiguing Kelso's overburdened mount.

Lynch said, "You think them Apaches will be any more help to us?"

"Not intentionally. They got back their own horses and they'll hide out until the Comanches go through. They don't want no part of them, if they can help it."

"If they took the Comanche horses, Piavah

123

will hunt them down."

Kelso said, "He'd try. But I'm thinking now that Algaday is too sly to take more than his own. He'd more likely leave the rest so's the Comanches wouldn't trouble to pursue him. He'd rather leave them the means to keep riding for Mexico.

"So they get their horses and they're on their Moon Raid trail again and we're right back where we started," Lynch said.

"Looks like it."

"Reckon I blew the big chance to rescue Annie, trying it alone. But I couldn't stand to see them bucks standing in line to take her."

"I already said I understood." Kelso directed his attention up ahead now, eyes and ears alert for sign of Piavah's bunch.

A series of yells broke the silence.

"Sounds like they found some of their horses," Kelso said. "Well, that tells us that they'll be riding on. And that we're on our own."

Lynch said, "Ever since they grabbed her out of Bonner, I've been remembering how they treat some of their women captives."

"She put up a fight when they took her, way it looked."

"That's what scares me," Lynch said. "They got devilish ways of taking that out of a woman like her."

"They were making her watch while they took the knife to you tied to that tree. Did you know that?"

Lynch looked dejected. "I saw her there. And more than anything else I wanted to act like a man in front of her. You once told me I was tough — had to be to live what I went through. But I never could stand torture — not like an Injun or a Mexican could. That comes from having to watch them torture other captives." He stopped, then said with shame in his voice, "I screamed more than once, in front of her."

"So did she," Kelso said. "When they slashed at your ear."

"She did?" Lynch's tone lifted. "By God, that shows she still has feeling for me! You see that, don't you?"

Chapter 10

The tracks of the Comanches showed they had recovered enough of their horses to be once more on their way. Except for the fact that they had left blankets and some gear at their campsite, the Kwahadies would have ridden south and left Kelso and Lynch far behind.

As it was, Kelso and Lynch nearly blundered head-on into a small party sent back to retrieve these left-behinds.

Just in time Kelso heard them coming and turned up a narrow side ravine, letting them pass. He counted nine of them, all leading extra horses.

Kelso said, "We've got to get you a horse."

Lynch slid down from behind the saddle. "Give me your knife," he said. "My kind of work."

Kelso handed the knife over. "What — ?"

"Wait here. I'll find you." And Lynch disappeared into the brush.

Kelso waited, once again musing over the Injun ways acquired by the former captive.

For all of Lynch's hatred of the Comanches, he was sometimes almost one of them himself. Kelso hoped this would help him now in what he had gone to do, whatever the hell that was.

Fifteen minutes later he heard a rider on the trail and went instantly alert. He drew his Colt and held it ready. The rider left the trail and entered the ravine.

The head of an Indian pony broke through the brush showing its single reined hackamore, and Kelso came almighty close to blasting its rider. He blew out his breath as he recognized Lynch.

Lynch rode close and handed him back his knife.

Kelso felt the wetness on the handle where Lynch had not quite wiped it clean. There was a fresh scalp tied by its hair to the pony's mane.

"You've got to be crazy," Kelso said in a low voice.

"I got a horse."

"Yeah. Let's ride." Kelso led the way out of the ravine and began following the trail south.

He kept wondering how Lynch had managed it. How had he waylaid one hapless Injun out of the bunch and taken time to scalp him, steal his horse and still slip away unnoticed? He had no answer. He shook his head.

Finally he said, "The others didn't notice?"

"Reckon not. Not yet."

Kelso shook his head again. But he rode in silence.

Lynch said, "The bastards got my saddle, well as my own horse, and they got them scalps I been taking off them." He sounded put out about this.

"Tough," Kelso said. "But we got more important things to think about."

"Yeah, I reckon."

"Every time you take one of their scalps, you're adding another hour's worth of torture if they get you again."

Lynch said, "They don't count it up that way. For what I already done, they'd give me the full treatment anyhow. Only I hope to God they don't get me again."

"A man who's scared of that treatment shouldn't never have took the vengeance trail," Kelso said. "What the hell were you thinking of when you started all this?"

Lynch didn't answer at once, then he said, "Don't guess I was thinking clear. But it's too late now."

"It is, for sure."

"If I can get Annie back, maybe I'll quit."

"Quit what?"

"Quit hunting scalps."

Once again Kelso held back from commenting that Lynch's future, once they got Annie back, if they did, was going to be a bleak one. Instead, he said, "I see you take easy to riding Injun style without a saddle."

"Done it a lot of years. But I miss a saddlebag. Maybe I could use yours?"

"What for?"

"To stick this Injun hair in. I wouldn't want to lose it."

"Not in my saddlebag you don't," Kelso said. After a pause he added, "I never had much use for scalp-hunters."

Lynch scowled. "Ain't like I was selling them to the Mex government like most do."

"That does make some difference. But the answer is still no."

"I got plenty of reason for what I'm doing."

"Maybe. Well, I got a reason for what I'm doing, too. You ain't stinking up my gear with no Injun's scalp."

"I was just asking," Lynch said.

Kelso dropped the subject and began to think of how they were going to move against the Comanches. He said, "That Apache chief told me about a Mexican village just below the border. Kind of a truce town where even enemy tribes mingle to trade without killing each other. Mexes, too. You ever hear of it?"

"Some."

"I wonder, was we to tackle Piavah there, could we dicker for the girl."

"Dicker what?"

"Might be something he wants more than her."

"There is," Lynch said. "Me."

"Besides you."

"Can't think what'd be."

"Yeah," Kelso said. "I reckon his tastes are simple: torture or rape."

"And raiding."

"Same thing," Kelso said. "All part of the simple, natural life."

"Them bucks may be having at her right now."

"Not unless they can do it on horseback," Kelso said. "She's safe while they're riding."

"It'll be dark soon," Lynch said. "And then what?"

"There'll be moonlight. They may keep going. If they stop, though, we'll have to pull off the trail. Don't forget that handful of braves behind us."

"If they stop, they may take up again on Annie," Lynch said.

Kelso swore. "We got to get her."

Lynch said, "One day I walked into the saloon there in Bonner and there she was. I never wanted any other woman since then."

Kelso could well understand how that could

happen. He said, "She's damn pretty, all right."

"I asked her to marry me, right off. At first she laughed at me. Then, later on, she kind of changed and I thought it was all set between us. And then — well, you know what happened then."

"She ran away from ranch life once. What made you think she'd take to it with you?"

"She was just a kid then. Full of a young girl's wish to know town life. I reckon she's seen her share of that now."

"Well," Kelso said, "you don't have a ranch anymore."

"I'll rebuild it."

"You don't have a life anymore, either."

"If I get a Texan jury, I'll go free," Lynch said. "And when I'm free, I'll come back and rebuild the ranch again."

"You forgetting Annie told you she didn't want to marry you?"

"That'll change," Lynch said stubbornly. "You'll see. When I get her away from them Comanches, she'll feel different. You can see how that could be, can't you?"

"Even if you went free, there'd still be Piavah."

"I intend to kill the sonofabitch."

"Yeah. Well, maybe we can do that," Kelso said.

As dusk fell it was hard to see in the canyon they had entered. The sides rose three hundred feet or more, and there'd not likely be moonlight in there for a while.

Lynch said, "You think they stopped up ahead?"

"If they broke out of this canyon into the open, they may keep riding."

"If they do, we'll lose them," Lynch said. "And hell, we can't stop here — we got that other bunch behind us."

"We'll keep on going."

Then, fifteen minutes later, they broke out into another valley, and a near-half moon gave them visibility.

"Here's where we turn off," Kelso said. "Them bucks behind us will be coming along. I don't want them on our back trail."

Lynch nodded and followed as Kelso skirted east along the escarpment for half a mile, then pulled up in an area of heavy scrub and took up watch for the rear detail of Comanches.

Halfway across the valley ahead, they could see a dark mass they judged to be the main bunch. And presently a smaller mass appeared from the canyon. That had to be the nine sent back to retrieve the gear — eight now, Kelso corrected grimly. The scalp of the ninth was hanging on Lynch's pony.

"They're all moving fast," Lynch said.

"They caught their horses quick enough," Kelso said. "That goddam Apache chief didn't waste much time scattering them. Probably grabbed his own mounts and hit for the back trails."

Lynch said, "No matter. The Comanches would have rounded up their ponies fast anyhow. They had plenty of practice."

Kelso was studying the dark blotches drawing closer together in the valley. He said, "Looks like they're stopping now."

"Makes sense. They'll camp there in the open. Less chance for a possible other attack by the Apaches."

"Ain't likely Algaday would take them on again, now he's got back his own horses."

"The Comanches will have guards out, just the same," Lynch said. "That'll make it hard to get near Annie."

"Make it damn near impossible."

"Any ideas?"

"Got to try a trick," Kelso said. "It's our only chance."

Lynch listened, frowning, as Kelso lined it out for him. Then he said, "I hope it works. Let's go."

Kelso had to admire the man's readiness to take the risk, knowing what would happen to him if he fell again into the Comanches' hands. He'd take any chance to free Annie;

133

he was hopelessly in love with her. And a hell of a lot of good that was going to do him, Kelso thought.

The trick had to be this: If there was one single thing about a Comanche that you could be certain of, it was that he was always horse-conscious. Horses to a Comanche were like gold or money to a white man. So they would work again on the horses.

The only objection brought up by Lynch had to do with the increased horse guard. "They lost their cavvy once to them Apaches. They're going to be watching them close now."

"Exactly," Kelso said. "And while they're concerned with the horses we're going to grab the girl."

"Hell, they won't all be with the horses."

"Maybe."

"What does that mean?"

"It means we're going to make sure they'll all be there."

"How?"

Kelso did not answer directly. "You know the Comanche lingo like one of them, don't you?"

Lynch said, "After all those years with them?"

"Then it's simple enough. All you've got to do is get near enough to the cavvy to sound like one of the guards, and yell out a warning."

"What'll I yell?"

"Yell that the Apaches are back. That they're making another try for the horses."

"What'll you be doing?"

"I'll grab the girl and run."

"You won't have much time. They'll find out quick enough that it's a trick."

"Time enough, I hope."

Lynch frowned. "I wish it was me was going to rescue Annie."

"Too bad, Sam. But you're the one can yell like a Comanche."

"If it works, you'll be the hero."

"Hero?"

"In Annie's eyes, goddammit!"

"Sorry, Sam," Kelso said, and meant it. "You ready?"

Lynch's face held a bitterness. But he said, "I reckon so."

It was still a couple of hours until first light, Kelso judged as they approached the Co-manche camp, dismounting and leading their horses the last half mile. A few hundred yards away they stopped to reconnoiter and pick out where the horse herd was held. The moonlight now made it easy to see.

"All right," Kelso said. "This is where we split up. Give me ten minutes to get close enough for the grab, then yell out your warning."

Lynch said nothing, only grunted once and slipped away.

Kelso moved a hundred yards nearer the quiet camp, then tied his mount in the brush and crept closer, slipping from cover to cover until he had a fair sight of the layout of sleeping figures.

That's when the big doubt hit him. How the hell was he going to pick out the girl?

At that moment Lynch gave his Comanche yell.

In seconds the camp was filled with startled, confused braves milling around, some armed but pointing aimlessly, not knowing where to fire.

And then Lynch yelled again, and they all took off at a run in the direction of the sound.

One figure remained alone, standing, and Kelso took a chance and ran openly toward it and saw that it was Annie.

She saw him coming and turned and started to run from him, and he called out her name.

She stopped then and faced him, and he reached out and grabbed her hand and tugged her along as he ran back to where he had left his horse.

Just as they reached it, a lone carbine banged away from the brush beyond the horse. Kelso dropped flat, pulling the girl down with him and drawing his sixgun at the same time. The Comanche was a lousy shot or they'd both be dead, he was thinking. And then the carbine flashed again and Kelso fired between the horse's legs and heard the Comanche scream once and then there was no more sound.

He got to his knees and crawled over to where he thought the Comanche was. Then he stood up and said, "Got him."

"Thank God!" Annie said.

Lynch came riding up fast, took in the scene and said, "You all right, Annie?"

"Sam?" she said. "Yes — I'm all right."

Kelso climbed up on his horse, and Lynch said, "We got no time to waste."

Kelso pulled the girl up to straddle behind his saddle, her dress lifting high. She seemed to take no notice of this, seemed stunned by the action of her rescue.

He thought she might fall, and half-turning his head, he said, "You'd best hang on to me," and took pleasure in his glimpse of her bared thighs.

She put her arms around his waist, clutching tightly.

He felt a response to this that made him glance over at Lynch, who was watching. Lynch's face was set and scowling. Kelso turned away and said in a low voice, "Let's ride."

"Where to?"

"We're getting off this Comanche Trail," Kelso said, "first chance we get." Up ahead they came quickly to an intersecting barranca, and he led the way into it.

"You better hope this ain't a blind canyon," Lynch said.

"I'm hoping."

"You ever been in this part of the rock pile before?"

"No. Have you?"

"No. It looks like the blind is leading the blind."

Kelso said, his voice rising, "You want to lead?"

"I couldn't do no better," Lynch said. "But if the girl bothers your thinking, she can ride with me."

"She don't bother me none."

"So I see."

Kelso looked over at him, and he could see the jealousy in Lynch's face. "It ain't nothing to bother you."

"Ain't it?"

Kelso didn't answer. There were dark shadows in the barranca bottom, and he strained his eyes trying to see if he had led them into a trap.

The silence between him and Lynch was charged and heavy enough to feel. And at that wrong moment, Annie seemed to recover enough to speak, and she said, "Thank you, Mr. Kelso. Thank you for saving me from those devils."

He saw Lynch stiffen and he met Lynch's bitter glance. Trying to take away some of the sting, he said, "There was two of us in on it, girl."

She went on, as if she had not heard him, "I'll always owe you for that, Mr. Kelso. What you did was a brave thing." She broke off in a stifled sob. "Oh, I couldn't have stood much more! Oh, God! I'm grateful to you." And she hugged him tighter and lay her cheek against the lean muscle of his shoulder and began to cry.

He stared straight ahead, unable to look again at Lynch, feeling Lynch's eyes burning on him. Damn the girl! She wasn't making it any easier between them.

But while he swore at her, he didn't really mean it. Not when he was feeling the press of her breasts against his back, the clinging of her firm, soft arms around him. It had been a long time since he'd felt a woman against him like that. A hell of a long time since he'd felt one as young and good-looking as she was.

He felt obliged, though, to speak again. He

said, "If it wasn't for Sam there, I'd never have made it. He done his part and more, too."

He felt her lift her head and heard her say, "Thanks, Sam. I'm grateful to you, too."

Lynch didn't answer her. Instead he must have rammed his heels hard into his pony's flanks, because the Indian mount gave a leap forward before he jerked it back roughly with the rein.

At this point they came to another intersecting canyon which angled in from behind and to their right. Kelso halted and stared at the ground ahead. It was daylight now.

"Now what?" Lynch said. "You better keep moving. Them Comanch may be on our trail. They'd find it plain enough at first light."

Kelso said nothing, just pointed.

"Well, what is it?"

"Look at those hoof prints coming from that other barranca. Mostly unshod. Injun horses."

"Piavah's?"

Kelso shook his head. "Not Piavah's. Algaday's, I'm thinking."

"Leastwise we ain't in a blind canyon then. Them Apaches know this country better than anybody."

"Don't get too relieved. That truce I had with the Apaches was only good until they got back their ponies."

140

"You think they'd turn on us now?"

"Why not? Haven't they always?"

"We could turn down the other canyon there. Go back out the way the Apaches came in."

"My thinking, too," Kelso said. "We can backtrack it to the Comanche Trail and be on our way home."

"Reckon there's water that way?"

"Something to think about. I got only half a canteen left."

"And I got none."

"Well, there's water holes someplace. Got to be a *tinaja* here and there that caught rainwater, if they ain't dried up or full of coyote droppings. Come on." He turned his horse into the other canyon.

Annie spoke up then and there was fear in her voice. "We won't meet up with those Comanches again, will we, Mr. Kelso?"

"I don't figure on it. Don't think they'll waste any more time on us. They got to be thinking mostly about their Moon Raid now." He was thoughtful, then said, "Any of them speak English to you?"

She hesitated before she answered. "One did. A wounded half-breed with curly hair."

"That's the one I call Chino."

"They say anything about their plans?"

Lynch was watching her and saw her blush.

She said, "Only their plans — of what they were going to do to me."

Lynch, quickly interested, said, "Did they?"

"Did they what?" Annie said.

"Did they do what they said they'd do?"

"What difference would it make?"

"That goddam Piavah!" Lynch said. "Kelso, I'm taking up his trail again."

"We made a deal," Kelso said. "Once we got the girl, you come in peaceful with me."

"But, dammit, man, you heard what she said they done."

"I didn't hear anything," Kelso said.

Annie said, "Thanks, Mr. Kelso." She looked at Lynch. "No, Sam. None of them did what they said. But they would have if you hadn't charged in single-handed two days ago — and got yourself caught. I'll always remember what you did."

Lynch said with a surly voice, "I'm glad to hear that."

Kelso said, "Sam, what we're going to do is this: As soon as we hit the main trail again we're taking it north — not south — and I'm taking you in."

He looked at Lynch then, knowing this had to be settled between them. He saw the rebellion in Lynch's eyes and held his hand ready near his sixgun, hoping it didn't come to that.

The tenseness suddenly left Lynch's body and he seemed to slump in defeat, and he said, "All right, then. I reckon I gave you my word. And I owe you — from last year. I won't fight you — over this."

Over this, Kelso thought. He wasn't sure what Lynch meant by that.

Chapter 11

They came out on the Comanche Trail and turned north and rode several miles in silence. Kelso was satisfied, even if Lynch was not. He was accomplishing his mission, and the girl was once again in safe hands.

His satisfaction was not total, of course. He still hated this job he had been sent on — to bring in Lynch. And his growing feeling for Annie, pleasurable though it was, was also disturbing. What could a Texas Ranger offer a woman?

He had enjoyed her admiration for what he had done in rescuing her, and he supposed that most men wanted the admiration of women. He also guessed that Annie knew this by instinct and could be using that knowledge for purposes of her own.

In his case he was not at all sure what that purpose was.

Had she really developed a feeling for him out of gratitude? Or was she using him to express to Lynch irrevocably that he was never, nor ever could be, more than a friend?

Kelso was uneasy, thinking about this. He did not like to be used. Moreover he felt sorry for Lynch. And he wasn't at all sure he wanted a permanent relationship with any woman. A ranger's life was hardly suited to such.

Still, Annie was a hell of an attractive woman, and if her gratitude went only to the extent of a temporary offer — Kelso felt a rising at the thought.

Anything more permanent than that — well, a ranger wasn't in a position to offer much. He was poorly paid and owned little more than a horse and a gun.

Sam Lynch, with his ranch, had set down roots, had wanted and offered marriage to the girl.

That showed how the plans of a man can go awry, Kelso thought. Maybe that's why he had never made any plans for himself. Well, Sam had nothing to offer now. Everything had gone sour for him. All on account of the impulsive whim of a Stone Age savage, Piavah.

So much for planning your life. It hadn't done much good for Lynch.

Lynch broke into his thoughts abruptly. "Dust up ahead," he said, and when Kelso looked he could see the faint rising like wispy smoke against the dun background of the rugged terrain.

His first thought was that Piavah had sent braves back along the trail looking for them, and that now they were facing them head-on. He discarded this idea almost as soon as he got it. Piavah wouldn't waste the time — he'd be getting on to Mexico. Or would he?

"We better get off the trail," Kelso said.

Lynch gave him an odd look. "Where you been?" he said. And he gestured at the sheer cliffs which rose on either side of them.

Only then did Kelso realize that while he had been musing about his possible relationship with the girl, they had entered a narrow barranca, which here was scarcely ten yards across and bare of all cover except a few scattered boulders.

He reined up, trying to decide what to do. He was trying to recall how far back it was that they had entered the defile.

As if in answer to his question, Lynch said, "We're five miles into this canyon, if you're thinking to turn tail and run for it."

"Horses couldn't stand it," Kelso said. "Not with one carrying double. And that dust ain't more than a couple miles away.

"And coming fast," Lynch said.

"You remember if this barranca widens out soon ahead?"

Lynch shook his head.

"Well, let's push on and hope to hell it does," Kelso said, and then wasn't sure this was a wise decision.

"I don't know about that," Lynch said.

Annie spoke up. "I do. I say do what Mr. Kelso says."

Lynch started to remonstrate, then suddenly shrugged. His face took on a bitter cast. "So be it," he said. "I won't argue with the both of you." Without waiting he kicked his horse and led off at a trot toward the nearing dust cloud, saying over his shoulder, "Maybe we can get out of this bottleneck in time to hide."

Kelso was already regretting his own decision, wondering if they'd do better to run before the approaching riders, hoping the horses would hold up. But with Lynch already moving on, angered by Annie's siding with him, he couldn't very well change his mind. Dammit! he thought, I may be letting the girl's presence influence my better judgment.

To make it worse, he now thought he remembered that this barranca stretched unbroken and steep-sided for maybe ten miles. If so, he'd got them trapped for sure. Suppose that dust was kicked up by stragglers from Piavah's band? Almost as bad could be another band of Mescalero Apaches. They had a sometimes habit of staking out whites in wet rawhides and letting the sun squeeze the life out of them. They weren't as vicious as the Comanches, usually, but they were bad enough. That rawhide game wasn't something that was played among friends.

"We ain't going to make it," Lynch said.

Up ahead now they could see that the towering sides of the barranca extended beyond the rising dust. Kelso cursed his earlier decision. If he'd had his mind on his job instead of on the girl — He said, "We'd better fort up here," and waved at a scattering of rocks a few yards ahead, insufficient to hide the horses, but big enough to afford some shield for a man — or a woman.

"You think they won't see us there?" Lynch said sarcastically.

"See us, yes. What I'm thinking of now is something between us and maybe bullets."

They halted and climbed down. Kelso said, "Annie, take the horses back a bit and get around behind that last pile of rocks. It ain't much but you'll be some away from any shooting."

She looked like she was going to object, then abruptly went away without a word. He called after her, "It gets bad, you run for it."

The two men took places behind the boulders, checking their guns.

Kelso said, "By their dust, I'd say there's

a half-dozen of them."

"We've got one chance," Lynch said. "You know that, don't you?"

"What's that?"

"Surprise. No words. If they're Injuns, when they get close, blast them."

"Chrissakes, they might not be Comanches, or even Apaches!"

"Down here, that ain't likely. And we got no time to waste identifying them. One quick look and we got to shoot."

"One quick look won't do it." Kelso looked over and saw Lynch had his eye sighted over his carbine barrel, ready for fast shot. "I'm telling you, Sam, don't shoot unless you got cause."

"You told us to keep riding this way, too," Lynch said. "Now look at us."

Annie's voice spoke from just behind them. She'd come back from where she'd left the horses. "Listen to him, Sam."

"You shoot and they turn out to be friendlies, you'll be in deep trouble," Kelso said.

Lynch snorted. "I'm in deep trouble now, ain't I? You're taking me in for murder. How much deeper in trouble can I get?"

"Plenty. Killing Comanches is one thing. Killing friendlies is something else." Kelso turned to the girl, "I told you to stay back there ready to ride."

She did not answer him. She said again,

"Listen to him, Sam. He's telling you true."

"Looks like you side him every time," Lynch said.

"He's right, Sam. Please?"

Lynch looked over to where she crouched now beside Kelso. "Two against one, again," he said. "Have it your way." Then, to Kelso, "God help us if you're wrong."

The hell of it was, Kelso thought, Lynch might be right. But even so, you couldn't just ambush strange riders because you think they might turn out to be enemies.

And then, as they approached, he saw they were white, five riders in range clothes. He glanced again at Lynch and saw him tensed as a coiled spring. He said in a whisper, urgently, "Don't do it!" and saw Lynch's jaw clamp tight in irritation.

When they were twenty yards away, Kelso called out, "Hold up there!"

The riders hauled up sharp, and the one in the lead called, "What goes there, friend?" He was solidly built, with blond hair showing below his hat, and a heavy, drooping mustache. His lips drew into a broad grin as he searched out the location of Kelso's voice.

Somehow, Kelso did not feel the grin reached the man's eyes.

He heard Annie's voice then, saying, "I know that one, Mr. Kelso. He came into the saloon in Bonner. I've danced with him."

Lynch said, "I remember the sonofabitch, too. He was bothering Annie the time I come back to see her after the Comanches butchered me."

"What is he?"

Annie said, "I don't know. Cowboy, he said. Army deserter, maybe. That was my impression."

"A regular around Bonner?"

"No. Only a couple of days. Came drifting through."

Kelso grunted. Then he called. "What's your name, friend?"

"Cole Rutledge, out of Pecos. Who wants to know?"

"You ever been in Bonner?"

"Up in the Panhandle? Sure."

"What's the name of the girl that sings in the saloon there?"

The blond rider's grin held fast while he appeared to be searching his memory. Then he called, "You talking about Annie? A damn good-looking piece of fluff?"

"What're you doing down here in the Bend?"

Rutledge's grin left him. "You're asking a lot of questions, friend. Now answer mine: who wants to know?"

"Kelso, Texas Rangers."

The grin came back. To the man's mouth anyway. He touched his heels to his mount and the horse moved forward. "That's different," he said. "Why didn't you say so? A man has got to be careful, riding down here."

"Answer the question."

"I come down to buy some Mexican cattle."

"Stolen?"

"You policing the Mexican side too, ranger?"

"No. Just curious."

Annie said, "Don't trust him, Mr. Kelso. I just remembered something else about him."

"What's that?"

"He beat up one of the other girls who works for Emory."

"That kind, eh?" Kelso said. He thought for a moment, then called to Rutledge, "Ride on by with your hands held high."

"No, I think not."

"You heard me."

"Damn peculiar acting for a law officer," Rutledge said. "Why don't you come out of hiding and show yourself?"

"I'll tell you once more. Do it my way."

Rutledge shrugged. "You got the drop. And you got the star — I guess." He turned in his saddle and called to his companions, "You heard what the man said."

Without answering, the four rode slowly

forward, hands held up in sight. Rutledge waved a hand as he went by the rocky cover. "Be more sociable if we all acted like friends," he said.

"Maybe," Kelso said. "But I ain't feeling sociable right now, maybe."

"Some other time, then," Rutledge said, still smiling.

Kelso said, "Just keep riding. The border is right ahead."

"I've got a familiarity with the border. Both sides of it."

"Kind of guessed that."

"Unfriendly cuss, for a ranger, ain't you?"

"Goes with the job. You ought to know why."

"You goddam rangers and the Mexican *Rurales* ain't much different."

"Save your compliments, and ride on."

They rode by, hard-set faces turned toward him, trying to search him out behind the rocks.

Rutledge was not grinning now. *"Kelso,"* he said. *"Kelso.* Now that's a name I won't forget."

"Don't come back."

Rutledge called over his shoulder, "Why, ranger, what reason would I have to do that?"

They watched the riders until they were out of sight. Then Lynch said, "What was the point of staying hid?"

"With five armed men against us two? Use your head."

"They may come back."

"What for?"

"Maybe because they'd be mad about the treatment they got."

"Not likely. Not when they got cattle business below the border."

"They might, though."

"Dammit! What else could I do? We'll push on hard, just in case, though."

Lynch said to Annie, "I don't like the idea of you dancing with that owlhooter, back in Bonner."

"It was part of my job," Annie said.

"I still don't like it."

"Dammit! Sam," Kelso said, "she didn't like it either."

"You don't know that."

"He was passing through Bonner when she met him. From where and to where? That's what I'm wondering. What business is he in?"

"Whatever it is, it ain't good. Kelso, we should have taken their canteens."

"That'd be a sure way to bring on a shootout."

"Suppose we don't find the next water hole?"

"A chance we take. Better than a five to

154

two gun fight, I figured."

"Against three," Annie said. "Mr. Kelso, I'm remembering something else about Cole. Something I heard after he left Bonner. Somebody saying he was handy with a long loop. That means rustler, doesn't it?"

"It damn sure does," Lynch said.

"Plenty of contraband cattle moving both ways through the Bend," Kelso said. "We all know that. Texas cattle stole and driven into Mexico. Mexican cattle stole and driven up to Texas. Take more rangers than we got to put a stop to it. We don't even try no more."

"What about the Army?"

"Hell, the contractors that supply the meat to the Army ain't particular where they get their beef. And Army brass ain't particular neither, long as they get their men fed." Kelso paused, then said, "Just because Rutledge is maybe mixed up in that, don't mean he'd come back just to get me."

"It's reason enough," Lynch said.

"Sam's right," Annie said.

It bothered Kelso that the girl had switched from backing his judgment earlier to siding with Lynch. Was she trying to play one of them against the other? On the other hand, he had to admit that there was some risk from Rutledge and his men.

Lynch said, "Ain't often an owlhooter will

155

pick trouble with a Texas Ranger. But this time, telling him you are one might have been wrong."

"My decision," Kelso said shortly.

Lynch nodded, then moved off toward where Annie had left the horses tied. In a few moments he was back, mounted on the Comanche pony and leading Kelso's. He said, "Their dust is far down the canyon. Reckon they're following your instructions. Let's hope they don't start getting madder and decide to come back."

"I'm betting they'll go about their business," Kelso said. "If they're on their way to a cattle deal, would they waste time trailing us?"

"Maybe not. They did talk like they had something going south of the border."

Kelso mounted with the girl, and they started northward again.

She said, her mouth close to his ear now as she held onto his belt, "I'm sorry I talked against you, Mr. Kelso." She paused. "But I'm afraid of Cole. He tried awful hard to get me to sleep with him. And when I wouldn't, he got that other girl to do it and the next morning she was covered with bruises. You know what I'm saying?"

Kelso said, "I don't have any use for a man who will beat a woman."

She let go of his belt then and put her arms

around his waist, and it seemed to him that she was holding him tighter than she had to. He wasn't sure about this, but he was sure that he liked the feel of it.

They had gone only a couple of miles when he heard Lynch's voice behind them. "Dust coming up the trail again. They're coming back."

Kelso reined his horse around to look. They were coming all right. He swore. "Well, we can't outrun them."

"You should have thought of that back there."

Kelso did not answer. He searched the cliffs around them. Just ahead there was a talus slide where the east rim of the barranca top had sluffed off. The foot of the talus raised the canyon bottom some twenty feet, over which the trail climbed, then dropped beyond.

He said, "We'll wait for them on the other side of the rise there. It's a hell of a better spot for a fight than we had before."

"Let's hope so," Lynch said.

They made the short climb and then the descent, and picketed the horses. The two men then climbed back up to the top and peered down the canyon. There was no doubt about it. The riders were approaching fast.

"This time we better shoot first," Lynch said.

"This time we will."

Annie came up and lay between them. She caught the implication of Kelso's words and gave him a strange look.

"You've changed your mind, Mr. Kelso."

"Like I said, I don't hold with a woman-beater." He turned his head and met her eyes, and he saw a warmth in them that started his pulse pounding. He said, "Best get back down a little. There'll be shooting soon."

She slid down the slope, but only a little way. She reached up then and put her hand on his leg as if to encourage him. He was glad that Lynch was intent on watching the trail and did not seem to notice.

They heard the shod hooves striking the rocky soil, and the pall of dust was close now. They sighted in on where they expected the riders to appear.

And then they heard a hard voice call down from above them, "Best lay down them rifles, gents. Hand guns, too. I got the drop on you for sure."

Kelso twisted slow and looked up at the top of the talus, and saw the barrel of a rifle poking over the rim.

The voice said, "Do it! I ain't going to miss from here."

They did as ordered.

The man on top gave a harsh laugh. "Reckon you gents didn't know there was another trail up here atop this mesa." He raised his voice and yelled, "I got them covered, Cole!"

Rutledge and the other three of his men rode out of the dust. Rutledge called, "Stand up and come forward. Annie, too. Yeah, girl, I got a look at you back there in the rocks as we rode by."

They did so and stood there, Lynch sullen, Kelso raging at himself for not thinking of a flank exposure from above, and Annie with her fear showing.

She said, "What do you want with us, Cole? We don't want any trouble with you."

Rutledge showed his mouth-only grin and said, "There's only one thing would put me to so much trouble. You ought to could guess what." He paused and his grin widened, but still did not reach his eyes. "There's you, girl. I always did have a strong hankering to romp with you. Maybe you remember?"

"I remember," Annie said. "But what do you want with a woman who doesn't want you?"

Rutledge laughed. "I won't bother now to tell you. Come nightfall, I'll show you. You know the saying — actions speak louder than words."

Lynch said, "You dirty rotten bastard!"

And Rutledge shot him in the leg.

Lynch went down, hit the ground on his side, and lay there. Blood gushed from a wound just above his boot top.

Annie cried out in rage. She ran toward Rutledge and clawed wildly at him as if to drag him from his saddle.

For a moment he sat there astonished. Then he swung his left fist and smashed it against her jaw, and knocked her down and out.

"I got me a she-cat to play with," he said. "And I'm looking forward to that." Then, "Two of you boys bring their horses over here and tie her on a saddle. And a couple gather up their guns."

The man on the rim came leading his horse down the steep, loose talus. One of the others said, "What about the ranger? You going to shoot him too?"

Rutledge was thoughtful. "No. I had a rule for a long time now: Never shoot a lawman, if you can help it. That applies even more so to a Texas Ranger. You kill one of them and it could bring a whole damn company of them scouring around down here."

He took the canteen from Kelso's saddle and dropped it to the ground. "Out of respect for the law," he said. "You go easy on that and you can make the spring up north ten miles or so. Don't try walking south after us — it's twenty miles to the nearest *tinaja*."

Kelso said, "What about him?" He gestured toward Lynch. "I need his horse to pack him in."

"Tough," Rutledge said. His face got bitter. "I should have put that bullet in his gut, the name he called me."

"Goddammit! I can't carry him."

"Leave him, then," Rutledge said coldly. "I'm taking both horses."

He gave a signal, and he and his men turned away, leading the Indian pony and Kelso's horse with Annie slumped in its saddle, her hands lashed to the horn. She was still groggy.

The sight of her that way sent Kelso to raging. The savage way that Rutledge had clubbed her with his fist fueled his hate, and he had a quick thought of what Rutledge had done to that other girl at Emory's.

He made his wild and desperate move then: a blind leap at the outlaw leader that surprised them all. He caught Rutledge by his rein hand and twisted and threw his weight onto it, dragging the man to his shoulder, and with a quick thrust he sent him somersaulting over it to slam against the ground.

That's when one of the others smashed a gun barrel down on his head and his brain exploded.

Chapter 12

He came to with the feeling that an axe had split his skull. He lay still, his eyes open but unable to see, his head throbbing with each beat of his heart. Then slowly his sight came back and with it his memory.

Painfully he rolled onto his side and saw Lynch sitting up, trying to tug his pant leg out of his boot top to expose his wound. He heard Lynch swearing steadily.

He crawled on his knees over to Lynch and looked at the wound. The slug had taken a chunk out of the fleshy high side of the calf, and maybe it had seared the muscle, but it had missed the bone.

"Can you stand?" Kelso said.

"I got to do more than that," Lynch said. "I got to walk."

"Yeah, me too. You hear what Rutledge said? About the spring? It's ten miles north."

"I heard," Lynch said.

"Nearest *tinaja* is twenty miles south. Walking, there ain't even enough water for one man to go that way. Going north, maybe one man could make it."

"So?"

"Wanted you to know."

"I know. You're going south," Lynch said, "after Annie. Things are changed some lately, ain't they? I seen how you been looking at her."

"What would you do?"

"Not what I *would* do. What I'm going to do. I'm going with you."

"On that leg?"

"If I lay here, I'll die," Lynch said. "You're going after her and that's the right thing to do. I got one chance — I got to go with you." He pulled a neckerchief from his pocket and tied it around his leg. The blood showed through immediately.

"I don't see how you can make it on that leg," Kelso said, watching as Lynch struggled to stand up.

"I'll make it," Lynch said. "Let's get started. All I got to do is think about Annie in the hands of that rotten sonofabitch." He met Kelso's eyes then and said, "You see the way she went after him when he shot me? That ought to tell you something. That ought to show you it's me she still wants, even if she don't know it her own self."

"Maybe." The idea didn't exactly please

Kelso. He got up and said gruffly, "Lean on me. Maybe up ahead I can find something to make you a crutch from."

They began to walk, slow and halting, Lynch breathing sharp with every step on his wounded leg. His weight pulled heavily on Kelso's shoulder, and at that moment it seemed near hopeless to him that they'd ever reach the *tinaja,* much less Cole Rutledge and the girl.

In two hours they made only four miles, Kelso guessed. They stopped for another rest and Lynch sank groaning to the ground, while Kelso stretched his cramped shoulder and studied the country ahead of the opening canyon. He was looking at a scorched sand waste, scattered with rocks, bristling with cholla and yucca and prickly pear. And after that, what lay ahead?

He heard Lynch's hard breathing and looked down and saw him stretched out on his back, his chest heaving too fast, his face too pale. "Desert ahead. We reach the edge, we'll cross tonight."

He unplugged the canteen and said, "Drink."

Lynch drank deeply, and where a moment before Kelso had urged this, he now grew impatient at the extent of Lynch's thirst.

He said, "Not all of it, dammit!" And then

he felt his own guilt as he raised the canteen to his own lips and drank nearly as much. They had to make it last, the worst still lay ahead. He said, "Sorry. But we ain't come a fraction yet toward that *tinaja* that bastard mentioned."

Lynch looked up from where he lay with his head dropped back into the sand. "We going to make it, Kelso?"

"We got to make it. Keep it in your head about Annie."

"I got it in my head," Lynch said, and sat up. He tried to rise and couldn't get his wounded leg under him. "Give me a hand up, this leg's got stiff on me."

Kelso stood looking at him with doubt.

"Dammit, man! Give me a hand up."

Kelso helped him up. There wasn't anything else he could do. If he left Lynch here, he'd have to take the canteen with him and the man would die before he could bring water back to him. If he left the canteen with Lynch, he'd never reach the *tinaja* himself. They'd have to make it together or not at all.

In mid-afternoon they came to the canyon end. He guessed it was ten miles across the desert flat, and ahead the brown, barren mountains were closer, but not by much. A cluster of close-growing yucca gave them a thin protection from the sear of the sun.

He rationed a mouthful of water to Lynch and one to himself, and they lay sucking at the dry air which seemed to have no life-giving to it.

He dozed off and came to with a start, hearing Lynch's voice in lunatic muttering. He guessed the man was delirious from exhaustion and pain, and then the words suddenly came clear and hard, although Lynch's eyes stayed closed.

"You and me, Kelso — we got to settle between us about her."

He did not know if Lynch was conscious when he said it, and right afterward he began to breathe easier and his muttering stopped and he seemed to be asleep.

It was dusk and the air was getting cooler when he awoke the second time. He shook Lynch and Lynch groaned and began to swear.

"We got to make some more miles," Kelso said, "while it's cool. Go as far as we can, long as we can see in the dark."

He got Lynch on his feet and they started off as before. The weight of Lynch against him was getting to be more than he could bear. He began to look wildly about him for some growth with sufficient limb to make a crutch. In all the miles they had come, there had been none. He set his jaw and forced himself to struggle on with Lynch sagging on his shoulder with every step.

Maybe, he thought, maybe there'll be some piñon up ahead when we reach the mountains. If we reach the mountains.

The waxing moon appeared as darkness came on them, and it lighted the trail.

"Like the sun, damn near," Lynch muttered. "Only without the heat."

"Comanche Moon," Kelso said. "Piavah will be raiding soon down Mexico way, maybe now, maybe a few nights from now."

"He started all this," Lynch said. "If I'm going to hang for killing Comanches, I'd like him to be one of them."

"Not much chance now."

"I can hope, can't I?"

Kelso plodded along awkwardly, Lynch's weight dragging at his strength. "You could say that you started it, too."

Lynch stopped and Kelso nearly let him fall. He stopped, too. "What the hell!"

"How you figure?"

"Good God, man, think!"

Lynch stood there, not moving for a time. Then he said, "I guess you're right," and reached out for Kelso's shoulder and limped forward, and they resumed their laborious way.

A long time later Lynch began to speak again, only now his half-delirium seemed to have returned. "Was Piavah started it. Everything was fine between Annie and me. Then he — I got to kill that sonofabitch before I hang." His voice was suddenly loud in Kelso's ear. "I got to kill him! You understand?"

"I know how you feel."

"Sure. Sure you do. You feel just like me — I been watching the way you look at her."

Kelso turned his head to look at him, but Lynch was staring straight ahead at the mountains.

At midnight Lynch collapsed, clutching at Kelso as he fell, dragging him down with him. They lay there a long time in the middle of the trail, too exhausted to move.

Later Kelso realized the danger of their exposure to possible attack and tried to shake Lynch awake. Lynch made no sound, and for a moment Kelso thought he was dead. And then he felt the rise and fall of Lynch's chest and grabbed him by the hands and dragged him off the trail and found a heavy growth of chaparral here.

The significance of this struck him now, and he raised his eyes to the south and saw the near outline of the mountains and knew they had crossed the desert flat and that the *tinaja* was somewhere in that range — if they could find it.

The moon, the Comanche Moon, was bright in his eyes as he fell asleep. He dreamed some time later that the moon caught fire from a flaming Comanche arrow, and he felt the scorch of its flames on his face and awoke holding his hands above him in protection. When he opened his eyes, squinting against the burn of it, he realized it was not now the moon but the sun which was high in the sky.

He woke up Lynch. "Let's go. We got to find that *tinaja*."

"Any water left?"

He shook the canteen and heard no sound. He was surprised; he was certain there had been a little left last night just after they had fallen in the trail. He looked at Lynch, his suspicion raging. "Goddam you," he said.

Lynch stared at him with eyes suddenly hot. "You think I drank it?"

"Who else?"

"Maybe you done it yourself, in your sleep."

"Like hell."

"You accusing me?"

Kelso could sense Lynch's rage growing to match his own. He fought to get a grip on himself, a fight that lasted for one long moment. Then he said, "Forget it. The water is gone. We best be getting on if we're going to reach that *tinaja*."

169

In spite of himself he could not keep from adding, "I was saving it for the final push."

"Then where is it?" Lynch said.

"I don't know."

Lynch said, "I do. Look on the ground where you flopped last night."

Kelso looked and could see the faintly darker spot in the sand. He bent down and pinched the soil and felt the moisture between his fingers.

"That's it, ain't it?"

Kelso's fingers went to the canteen cap and found it was loosened on its threads. He was swiftly chagrined. Had he forgotten to screw it on tight after the last drink they had shared? Let the precious mouthfuls they needed to reach the *tinaja* seep away while he slept? His rage was now directed at himself.

"That's it, ain't it?" Lynch said again.

It was hard to say, but Kelso said it. "That's it."

"I ain't happy to hear that. But I like it better than being the one accused."

"Sorry," Kelso said. "I reckon I'm drawed out tighter than a bob-wire fence."

He felt Lynch's glare on him, and then Lynch leaned his weight on him again and together they started on, the empty canteen banging against Kelso's hip on the opposite side, reminding him of his mistake at every step.

They left the chaparral and the trail entered arroyo-slashed foothills. The sun in here was even hotter and more oppressive than it had been on the desert. There seemed to be no air at all.

Above and beyond the hills, they could see the stark side of the mountain itself. There had to be a gap there somewhere. And there had to be a water tank. There had to be, unless Cole Rutledge had been lying.

They stumbled on, and then they came to a faltering stop.

Lynch slid to the ground, his grip loose, and Kelso made no try to stop him. Kelso was staring ahead. He blinked. His throat was so dry that he could only croak. "There," he said. "There!"

To one side of the trail was a vague patch of green among the dun-colored rocks and sage.

Lynch said nothing. Kelso looked down and saw he was out cold. He lifted his eyes again to that green target up ahead and moved jerkily toward it. At first the splash of color seemed to retreat so that its distance held. Then slowly, slowly, he drew closer.

And then he was there, and in a narrow ravine there was a tiny stand of cottonwoods, rising above a screen of brush.

He was suddenly trying to run, stumbling,

falling to his knees, getting up and plunging recklessly through the bushes and into the trees beyond.

And there it was, a shallow basin carved by erosion into the surface of a large, flat rock. From a crevasse in the rock cliff above dripped a seepage of clear water from some unknown storage inside the mountain.

The caught water was filmed with floating insects, and around it were the droppings of animals, but Kelso threw himself prone, plunged his face below the surface and swallowed heedlessly.

He filled the canteen and brought it to Lynch, then helped him to the *tinaja*. They rested there in the shade of the cottonwoods, but now that their thirst was relieved, their hunger grew. It had been a long time since either had eaten.

Kelso prodded Lynch. "Get up. We got to move away from here."

Lynch groaned. "Why?"

"We got to get game."

"How?"

"This place is lousy with javelina hoof prints. This has to be where they water. But they won't come around while we're here."

"How you going to get a javelina without a gun?"

"Come on," Kelso said, without answering.

With Lynch clinging to him again, he worked their way a short distance up the mountain. Then he said, "Those little wild pigs get thirsty enough, they'll maybe not bother with the smell we left at the *tinaja*."

Lynch was clutching at his wounded calf. "Climbing up here ain't helped my leg none."

"You rest here. I'm going higher. There's piñon growing up there. I'll cut limbs from one. I got to make a crutch for you."

"A crutch?"

"Yes, goddammit. I can't carry you no more."

"All right," Lynch said, and sprawled out uncomfortably on the mountainside.

A half-hour later Kelso came down with a couple of piñon limbs, one short and heavy, the other lighter and forked at one end to form a crude crutch.

There was nothing left to do then except wait and hope.

It was late afternoon before he heard them returning down below. Lynch was sleeping out his exhaustion. Kelso arose quietly and stole his way down toward the *tinaja,* carrying the club he had fashioned out of the short limb.

He crept close, still hid in the brush and saw a half-dozen javelinas wallowing at the edge of the shallow tank. They grunted and shoved at each other, all bristles and tusks, their small hoofs sounding on the rock rim of the basin.

He debated trying to get one with a throw of the club and discounted his chances. They were too tough for that. He had to rush them, take his chance up close. He felt a moment of sweat then. They were small, but when excited and cornered, they could fight viciously. They could rip a man's legs to ribbons with those tusks.

He sprang toward them and, blocked by the cliff behind the *tinaja,* they turned and charged straight at him, the discharge from their musk glands stinking the air around them. One of them caught his pant leg, shredding it but missing his flesh. He swung down hard with the club and caught the beast across the spine and broke it. The javelina squealed its agony once, then threshed wildly, crawling with its hind quarters dragging, lunging with its tusks, trying till the last to slash him.

Kelso swung again and again at the tough little boar, slowly clubbing it to death. When it lay still finally, he felt ready to retch, and not only from the stink of it, either.

"Enough to knock the appetite right out of a man," he muttered. He drew his knife and cut out the musk glands. When he looked up he was startled to see Lynch standing there,

174

the piñon crutch under his armpit.

"Man, the noise you was making, I thought you'd took on the whole Rutledge gang single-handed."

"I damned near rather," Kelso said. "Let's get a fire going. It'll take some cooking to make this tough little bastard chewable."

When they started out again, they moved better, refreshed by the water and the food, and Kelso no longer having to support Lynch's weight.

The trail was still broadly defined. Even though it climbed the rising floor of a narrow gap, there was enough moonlight filtering down to show the way.

But near the middle of the night fatigue overtook them again, and they halted. At this higher altitude, and without blankets, the cold made sleep fitful for them despite the fire of brush and small limbs they built.

"Fry all day and freeze all night," Lynch said, throwing more branches on the flames. "You think we'll ever find them outlaws, Kelso?"

Kelso thought for a moment, then said, "That town the Apache chief told me about. San Carlos, the trading town. If Rutledge is buying contraband cattle, seems likely that's where he'd do it."

"We got to get guns before we tackle him."

"I got expense money left," Kelso said. "They never shook us down for cash. I got enough for guns anyway, and a couple of horses."

"Where's this San Carlos?"

"Algaday said it ain't far off the Comanche Trail, west branch. I figure that's the branch we're on now. If we keep to the right of that next mountain range, we ought to come pretty close."

Lynch studied the black silhouette of peaks against the moonlit sky to the southeast. "I hope it ain't as far away as it looks," he said. "This is a hell of a country for a one-legged man."

Chapter 13

San Carlos lay a dozen miles south of the Rio Grande. It had been built originally by the Spanish as an outpost against the Indians of what was to become Texas.

For years it remained just that, usually garrisoned by the dregs of first the Spanish and then the Mexican army. Often convicted criminals were given the choice of enlistment for duty in the outpost instead of prison or death. The officers sent to command these convict-troopers were seldom more commendable than those they commanded.

And sometime during the later years, an arrangement had come into existence between these corrupt officials and the Indian tribes they had been sent to protect against. By this arrangement San Carlos became a truce town. Indians who were pressed by enemies, white or red, were given refuge there. In turn they agreed never to molest the people of San Carlos, although they were free to raid in all other parts of Chihuahua. And, of course, Texas.

Before long the people and soldiers and crooked officers of San Carlos were trading with the renegades, first red then white, too, for stolen stock, kidnapped persons and contraband of all kinds.

It was a profitable situation which endured because of an inviolable rule accepted by all races: There was not to be any warfare among those refuged there.

Thus, as Algaday had told Kelso, traditional enemies mingled with impunity, traded among themselves and with others. The key word was profit.

Away from the town one tribe might slay the other, or Mexican might kill Indian, or Indian raid other Chihuahuans, but in the vicinity of San Carlos, there was always a tense, superficial peace, a situation much like the uneasy accord that existed for decades between the Comanches of Texas and the Mexican and white Comancheros of Santa Fe.

Kelso was not sure he and Lynch would qualify for the protection accorded the mixed bag of border-jumpers. Certainly not from Cole Rutledge and his bunch, or from Piavah and his Comanches if they were in the area.

It was near dark when he and Lynch straggled into the town. All afternoon they had waited a few miles outside of it, shielded by scant chaparral, suffering again from thirst, worried about what they were getting into.

If there was authority in San Carlos, and there must be, Kelso reasoned — you couldn't just have anarchy — it had to come from the military, or possibly, the dreaded Rurales.

Porfirio Díaz, the Mexican dictator, had formed the Rurales soon after he took power. He had originally patterned them after the Texas Rangers. But the almost autonomous power he gave them in order to maintain a semblance of law in the desolate Mexican back country had grown out of hand. They did keep order of a sort, where and when they wanted to. They kept it by taking over the powers of police, judge and jury, and executioners. A trial by Rurales seldom lasted more than a few minutes. It was a short time from the moment of arrest to the time of ready for burial. Most peons lived in terror of these tough and cold-eyed dispensers of the law.

There had been occasional confrontations between Rangers and Rurales, and these almost always occurred south of the border.

Legally, here, the Rangers were at fault, because they had no right to enter the sovereign territory of Mexico, whether after border-jumping renegades or for any other reason. Rangers on a hot pursuit were apt to conveniently forget this. But the Rurales never did.

No, Kelso thought. Avoid contact with the Rurales if at all possible.

San Carlos was all weathered, scarred adobes and dirt streets, a crude and dirty town without refinements. There was a small unkempt plaza with a few wilted, dusty trees. There were cantinas everywhere, and painted Mexican girls in short, tight skirts. Men quarreled here individually and some died here, but there were no full-scale wars. Small differences could be settled here, but big differences were settled elsewhere, out in the deserts or the mountains and on the mesas, or in the gorges cut by the Rio Grande.

Here was where Kelso hoped to find Cole Rutledge or find word of him — and of Annie.

Here is where Rutledge must have been headed when he spoke of traveling south to make a deal for cattle.

The thought of Annie made him increase his pace.

Lynch remonstrated. "Wait up. I'm on a crutch, goddammit!"

"I was thinking of Annie."

"Me, too. But I can't run on this forked stick."

Kelso slowed to a more reasonable walk.

"You going to be able to get around without it?"

"Why?"

"You stick out like a sore thumb that way."

"My leg feels like a sore thumb — a big one."

"Get rid of the crutch if you can."

"I reckon I can limp along without it. The wound is scabbed over and so far there ain't any infection. Just sore as hell."

"Good."

Lynch threw aside the crutch, and they were soon caught up in the movement of the natives along the narrow streets.

They stopped at one of the first cantinas they came to and turned in and sat at a table and each ordered beer.

Almost at once a *puta* came up to them, her high cheekbones heavily rouged. Still, she was pretty and brown with unfathomable black eyes and white teeth.

She offered herself to Kelso for two pesos, and when he shook his head, she looked at Lynch. The woman's eyes fixed on his scarred head, which she seemed to be noticing for the first time in the dim light of the cantina.

Lynch waited, a cynical hard smile on his lips, and when she turned away without soliciting him, he said bitterly, "There you are. Even a goddam Mexican whore won't have nothing to do with me, on account of me being scalped."

Kelso didn't know what else to say, so he said, "We got to buy you a hat."

With their thirst satisfied, Kelso led the way to a restaurant a few doors down the street. They ordered a meal and looked around.

There were three Mexican army officers at a rear table, and at another table near them four Rurales were splitting a bottle of mescal. The rest of the patrons were a mixture of Americans and Mexicans, mostly in range garb, although there were a few better dressed who appeared to be town traders.

Receivers of stolen goods was more likely, Kelso thought. There seemed to be plenty of money floating around, so trading must be prospering.

It was the Rurales that bothered Kelso the most. They were all big felt sombreros, short charro jackets and mean-roweled spurs.

They looked as mean as their spurs, in a quiet, tough sort of way. Even without the eagle-and-snake insignia they wore on the jackets, you would have known what they were.

Halfway through his meal Kelso looked up to catch one of the Rurales staring at him. Across the dimly lit room he thought he saw a sudden, quickly hidden show of recognition on the Rurale's hard-tempered face. At the same time he had a vague feeling of having seen the Rurale somewhere in the past.

Kelso looked back at his plate, thinking about this. He couldn't place the man, but the familiarity of his features nagged him. He looked up again and the Rurale was still staring at him. Kelso met his stare and they held that way for a long moment, and then the Rurale turned toward one of his companions and said something to him. The other Rurale did not look around, but his lips moved in answer.

Kelso said to Lynch, "We better get out of here."

"I ain't through," Lynch said. "And this is the first full meal we've had in weeks."

"Come on."

Outside the restaurant Lynch said, "Well?"

Kelso started walking toward the center of the town. He said, "That big Rurale — I just remembered something about him."

"What?"

"Couple of years back there was some trouble around El Paso. Mexican bandit named Ibanez raided on our side, killed a couple of men. Four of us rangers picked up his trail and went right after him into Mexico, which ain't legal, of course. We caught up with him in the little town of Guadalupe. We took Ibanez and three of his men after a shoot-out in the plaza where we killed two others of his gang. We started back north, moving fast with our prisoners, and right behind us come a couple of Rurales, mad as hornets because they'd missed the whole action in their plaza. We had a confrontation on the trail, with the Rurales demanding that we give up the prisoners, and with our Ranger captain refusing. I remembered there in the restaurant that one of those Rurales was the same one I was looking at at that table in the back."

"He recognize you?"

"I think so. If so, he'd sure like to make trouble for me, I'll bet. We refused to give up those bandits to him that time. And being outnumbered four to two, he had to back down, and I think that was the worst of all for him. It ain't often a Rurale has to back down from anybody. They're the toughest sonsofbitches in Mexico, and it hurt his macho something terrible when we took Ibanez and his raiders back across the Rio to stand trial in Texas. The last time I saw that Rurale he was standing this side of the river watching us cross, and he had murder in his eye."

Lynch said, "Hell, he was in the right, wasn't he?"

Kelso said shortly, "All in the way you look at it. If we hadn't done what we done that sonofabitch Ibanez would still be raiding and killing Texans and jumping back safe into Chihuahua." He paused. "Well, we caught some hell from the adjutant-general's office, and our captain had to resign from the Rangers, but I never regretted none of it."

"You may now," Lynch said, "if that Rurale decides to get even with you."

"My thought exactly," Kelso said. "And without guns we wouldn't stand a chance. We got to find a store and buy some, and some clean clothes, too."

A little farther on they came to a *tienda de ropa* that sold both clothing and weapons, and Kelso turned in. They each picked out a Colt, a holster and gun belt, a Winchester carbine and ammunition.

Then they turned their attention to replacing their clothing. It was little wonder that the Rurale had stared at them, Kelso thought. Possibly he had not recognized Kelso at all. He might have been merely curious about the blood-stained clothes. Maybe, but not likely.

"Now we got to hnd a *posada* to stay at," Kelso said, "while we try to find out if Cole Rutledge is around and what he's done with Annie."

They found a hotel on a back street of the bustling town. "For the size of the place there's a lot of coming and going," Kelso said.

Even at this hour after dark riders were coming and going. Here and there he even spotted a few Indians, squatting or standing in stolid watchfulness. He wondered if any of them were Comanches, and decided against this. Any Comanches would be with Piavah, wherever he was. Unless they were some who had defected from Quanah years back, always a possibility.

Apaches? Possibly. Who knew where Algaday might show up next?

He wondered what would happen if he ever crossed trails again with the Apache leader. Their brief alliance had been one of the Apache's whim, and it had not been altogether successful from Kelso's standpoint. He'd guess that if they met again it would be as enemies. After all, Algaday had told him that he hated Texas Rangers more than most whites.

He had more immediate problems to think about. He had to find Annie, and he had to try to get her away from Cole Rutledge. Had Rutledge already tired of her? Maybe disposed of her, one way or another? A sinking sensation caught at his gut. A man who beat women for pleasure — he was capable of anything.

And where was Rutledge? Was he in San Carlos or was he somewhere farther south?

That's what he and Lynch had to find out first.

Right now, though, they both needed rest. But first they would take advantage of the hot tub baths offered by the fat Mexican *posadero*. He was a waddling, smiling mountain of a man, all geniality and without apparent curiosity, a thing which could be disturbing. Two trail-beaten and blood-stained gringo guests should have excited some speculation, it seemed to Kelso. Unless such a sight was common in San Carlos, and this was possible, too.

Now fed, bathed and reasonably clean-dressed, they turned in, only their boots off and with sixguns under pillows. Within minutes they were sleeping out their exhaustion.

In the morning they sought out another restaurant, and Kelso was relieved that they did not encounter the Rurale who had stared at him the previous night. As soon as they breakfasted, they went out to look for sign of Rutledge and the girl.

In daylight the town had more bustle than it had at night. Wagons filled with unknown cargo came in, unloaded in front of stores or warehouses, sometimes loaded with other merchandise and pulled out. Riders came and went. Indians walked the streets with gringos dressed for the range and charro-clothed Mexicans.

Kelso had read somewhere of a cosmopolitan city in the East, and the description came to his mind as he looked about him. That's it, he thought. San Carlos is a *cosmopolitan* town, *cosmopolitan* meaning the biggest collection of red, white and brown-skinned outlaws ever gathered in one place.

He wondered grimly how much of the contraband that passed through the town came from Texas. Seeing San Carlos as he was seeing it now was an eye-opener for a Texas Ranger.

It was something to remember for the future. If there was any future. He was on dangerous ground here, especially if that damn Rurale had recognized him from the time in Guadalupe.

They gravitated to the dusty plaza around which the town was built. Kelso figured it might be the place to pick up information. The plaza was where those who seemed apart from the hustle of the town loafed in the sun or the shade according to the temperature of the hour. Here there were *viejos,* old men who existed God knows how, and who might be approachable, or who might be heard gossiping among themselves if a Spanish-speaking gringo listened hard enough.

But he was disappointed. A half hour

passed, and he knew from the bits of desultory conversation that passed between the idlers, that though they talked among themselves they said nothing. Nothing of the town's business nor of the town's businessmen. Nothing of the trade or the traders. The idlers had learned a long time ago that silence concerning the affairs of San Carlos was the way to survive. A *viejo* did not gossip of anything of importance in San Carlos. A loose mouth could mean quick death.

Kelso could feel all this without being told. He could tell it by the way the *viejos* ignored his and Lynch's presence, as if they were invisible.

Once he tried to strike up a conversation with an ancient-faced peon who sat on a stone bench near them.

"*Dígame,* old one. Tell me, how does one go about finding a friend whom one was to meet here in San Carlos?"

The old one kept his eyes straight ahead, not looking at Kelso, and his lips scarcely moved as he answered in a low voice, "One should meet him at a prearranged place."

"But if no prearrangement was made?"

"Then the one you want to meet was not a friend," the old one said, and got up and moved away.

Lynch, who had not understood the words,

guessed by the tone what had passed between Kelso and the old man. He said, "No luck?"

Kelso shook his head, but said nothing. His eyes were on the rider who had just approached the plaza and now turned into it, brashly putting his mount onto the walkway leading to the benches. It was the Rurale who had studied him the previous night in the restaurant.

The Rurale halted in front of them and sat looking down, a faint, cold smile showing. He said, in fair English, "Do you know me?"

Kelso said, "Should I?"

The Rurale ignored the question. "My name is Mata. To remember the name, think of the Spanish word for 'kill'. As in *matador*. It would be well for you to remember that, because I am the *jefe* of Rurales around San Carlos and I do not like Texas Rangers south of the border." His smile widened but did not get warmer. "For that matter I do not like them north of the border, either."

"I'm sorry to hear that."

"My dislike dates from that time at Guadalupe."

"Ah, Guadalupe!" Kelso said.

"So now you remember, eh?"

"I remember. But it is best forgotten."

"It is not a thing that a man like me forgets," Mata said. His forced smile faded. "What are you doing here in San Carlos, ranger? Your

190

authority ends at the river, although you *hijos de putas* don't seem to understand that."

"I'm not here as a ranger," Kelso said. "A woman of mine was kidnapped by a gringo rustler named Cole Rutledge. I come to find her."

Mata looked at Lynch, who was scowling. "And you?"

"The woman is mine," Lynch said, with some heat.

Mata flashed a grin which went quickly. "It's like that, eh? Two rivals for one woman." He shook his head. "That makes for bad trouble."

"Have you seen the woman here?" Kelso said. "A good-looking *muchacha* with brown hair and hazel eyes."

"There are many whores here in San Carlos."

Lynch jumped to his feet.

The Rurale said, "Easy, gringo. I am a *pistolero* of some reknown. I could take you easily."

"She is not a whore," Lynch said.

Mata kept his eyes on Lynch but spoke again to Kelso. "So she is not a whore. Well, we don't get many of that other kind here. Taken by the gringo Rutledge, eh?"

"Is he here?"

"And if he is?"

"I am here to get the girl back."

"Get out of San Carlos," Mata said. "Get out of Mexico. You goddam rangers have no rights this side of the river."

"When I get the girl."

Mata studied him, suddenly thoughtful, but without losing his resentment. "All right," he said in a confidential tone, his words shaded with a strange reluctance. "I will tell you where you can find Rutledge. He has a herd of three hundred cattle bunched in the holding graze south of the town."

Kelso said, too quickly, "Gringo-owned cattle?"

Mata smiled coldly. "Always the ranger, eh? No, not gringo. Mexican. Traded to him by Mexican thieves. Rutledge will drive them north to your Fort Davis and sell them to your Army suppliers there. Your Army will be eating beef stolen from Mexicans. You see why we do not like gringos?"

"I see why you tell me where to find Rutledge," Kelso said cynically. "If I should eliminate Rutledge, you would, of course, return the cattle to the rightful owners."

Mata's smile became a grin, but his eyes stayed hard. "Of course, ranger. I'm an officer of the law, just like you are."

"South of the town," Kelso said. "How long have they been there?"

"Only since yesterday. Rutledge will move them northward tomorrow. These operations move fast through San Carlos."

"Thanks for the information," Kelso said.

"*Por nada,* ranger. As one lawman to another."

"Yeah," Kelso said. But he didn't believe it.

Mata flicked his eyes from one to the other of them. He shook his head. "Think of it," he said. "Two *amigos* in love with one woman. *Mucho* trouble."

Chapter 14

The holding area for stolen cattle was a wide, flat plain a few miles to the south of San Carlos. Kelso and Lynch found a livery stable where the owner sold them a couple of fair riding mounts and worn Mexican saddles. They hadn't the time to shop around for better. For all they knew Mata himself might send word about them to Rutledge. Kelso mistrusted the Rurale chief. It had to be something more that induced Mata to tell of Rutledge's whereabouts.

As they rode toward the plain, Lynch said, "So this is Rutledge's business. He rustles or buys stolen cattle and sells them to Army suppliers. You think the Army buyers don't know they're stole?"

"No questions asked, most likely. As long as the cattle carry a Mex brand."

"And the Rurales wink at what's going on?"

"Must get their cut. Which makes me wonder about Mata. He's got no reason to do me a favor."

"I was thinking the same."

"Of course, with Rutledge out of the way he could take over — have his own men drive the cattle north, make his own deal at Davis."

"Wouldn't put it past him none," Lynch said.

"Still, in the long run, he might be the loser by it. The way it is now, I'd guess he gets a regular cut out of every herd goes through here. And it costs him no effort. Why would he spoil a good thing like that?"

It was something to think about. Where did Mata really figure in? Was he the big law in San Carlos? Did he have more clout than, say, the officer commanding the small Mex army garrison, whoever he was? It seemed likely that such an officer would demand a cut of the trade. He would want his *mordida,* his bite, as the Mexicans called it.

There was a lot he didn't know about the control in San Carlos, Kelso thought, and his ignorance could mean big trouble for him. But he didn't have time to waste learning. He was afraid that even now he was too late.

Too late, certainly, to save Annie from more brutality than any woman could be expected to endure. She had already suffered at the hands of the Comanches. How much could she stand without breaking? Maybe she had broken already.

She was tough, he had to admit. But there was a limit to what even she could take.

Suddenly he saw the herd ahead. A creek lined with willows crossed the grassland here, and next to the trees in the distance he could see a chuck wagon of sorts and a small cluster of horses and men. Here and there other riders kept an eye on the herd itself.

"He had four men, back in the Bend," Lynch said. "Now he's got an army."

"Hired *vaqueros*, I'd guess," Kelso said. "Trail drivers. They may or may not be *pistoleros*."

"You suppose he's got Annie in that wagon?"

"Ain't likely. Scarce be room enough if the wagon is carrying chuck for all them men."

"How we going to find out?"

Kelso sat in silence, not able to think of a way. Then suddenly, a group of five near the wagon mounted up and headed north toward where Kelso and Lynch were hidden by a rock-thrusted hillock which sloped eastward to the creek.

"There's your answer," Kelso said. "That's Rutledge himself and his gun men. Heading into town, I'll bet. And leaving them vaqueros to mind the herd."

"We could ambush the bastard right here," Lynch said.

"And maybe never find out where Annie is. Even if we could take the whole five of them." Kelso led his horse back down the rise so they wouldn't be skylined when they mounted up.

He moved then toward the creek at a fast walk, in a hurry to reach it before Rutledge reached the gap through the low hills, and yet fearful of kicking up dust which could give them away.

They rode into the screening of willows and looked back and saw Rutledge and his men continuing northward toward the town, and Kelso breathed his relief.

He immediately turned south down the creek edge, heading to where they had spotted the wagon and the vaqueros, but staying in the fringe of trees.

"Suppose they are *pistoleros?*" Lynch said.

Kelso shrugged and said nothing. They could glimpse the wagon through the trees now, a hundred yards away. Kelso dismounted and Lynch did likewise. Kelso handed him his reins and said, "Wait here. I'm going to try to sneak close enough to get a look inside the wagon." He started to move off, and Lynch grabbed his arm with his free hand.

"Better let me do the creeping and crawling. Living with them damn Comanches taught me something. I make a damn sight sneakier Injun than you do."

Kelso had to admit that was true. What was it somebody had said? That Lynch was half-Comanche himself in some ways? "All right," he said. "But no showdown with them vaqueros if we can help it."

"Dammit! I know that," Lynch said exasperatedly. "That's the reason I'm going. But if Annie's in there, I'm taking her out, no matter what."

"Understood," Kelso said. "And if it comes to a shooting, I'll be there pronto."

"Make it faster than that," Lynch said, and was gone.

Ten minutes later he came back, frowning. "She's not there."

Kelso raised a hand in signal for silence. He stood listening, then said, "Wait here. I've got a feeling." A moment later he was across the creek and slipping into hiding on the opposite side in a thicket of willow.

He waited expectantly, and then he knew his hunch was right. A vaquero came riding slowly up the creek, his eyes picking out the boot prints of Lynch in quick glances as he came warily watching ahead for sign of his quarry.

So Lynch hadn't been as Comanchelike as he supposed, Kelso thought. He shot a quick look behind the tracker to make sure no others followed, then raised his Winchester and said, "*Manos arriba!* amigo! Raise your hands!"

The vaquero stopped his horse in its tracks and his hands shot up, stretching his bare wrists far beyond the sleeves of his tight charro jacket. He sat rigid in his saddle, he did not even seem to breathe.

Lynch heard Kelso's voice and came walking cautiously, leaving the horses ground-hitched where they stood. When he saw the vaquero under Kelso's gun, he halted. Then he walked up to the Mexican and said, "Your gun, amigo."

The vaquero understood the extended palm, if not the words. Very carefully he drew his pistol from its high-worn holster and held it out between his thumb and forefinger. He said nothing.

Kelso waded back across the shallow creek, keeping his eyes on the man. When he was a few paces away, he said in Spanish, "Get down, amigo. I want to speak with you."

The Mexican got down, his face inscrutable as an Indian's. And why not? Kelso thought, he's got the face of a Yaqui.

The vaquero said, "Speak by all means, señor. Believe me, I am listening."

"Your *patrón*, he is Señor Rutledge?"

The Yaqui nodded.

199

"He has a woman with him? A gringa?"

The Yaqui did not answer at once. Then he sighed and said, "She is not here, señor."

"Where?"

"In San Carlos."

"And where is she kept in San Carlos?"

"At night she sings in the Cantina Flores."

The reply started Kelso. When he spoke again, he said, "Perhaps we are speaking of different women —"

"The gringa woman of Señor Rutledge that I know of, she sings every night at the Cantina Flores," the vaquero said.

Lynch said to Kelso, "What's he saying?"

Kelso told him and Lynch said, "That's a damn lie — a *mentira!*"

The vaquero said, "No, señor, no *mentira*. I do not lie when two guns are pointed at me. Although I am a very brave man, I am not stupid."

Kelso said, "The gringa is kept prisoner by Rutledge during the day?"

"In the *cárcel,* the jail. The *jefe* of Rurales, Mata, has her under lock and key, señor. At night she is let out to sing."

"Why?"

The Yaqui shrugged. "I do not know. It is an arrangement between them."

"How long has this gone on?"

"A few days, I understand. Ever since Rutledge came down from Texas to wait for the cattle we have driven up for him. Tomorrow he will drive the cattle north and we will return south. That is all I know, señor."

"You do not work for Rutledge?"

"No, señor. I work for Chato Carmona, who is well known in Chihuahua. He sells cattle to Rutledge and Rutledge drives them north."

"A well-known *bandido,* this Carmona," Kelso said.

"A matter of opinion, señor. He has the reputation, but the gringo Rutledge is more thief than Carmona."

"I would not argue that."

"What the hell is he saying?" Lynch said impatiently.

Kelso relayed a few words.

"What happens to Annie when Rutledge goes north?" Lynch said.

Kelso queried the vaquero.

"I have heard he will sell her to the owner of the cantina," the Yaqui said. "That is why she is let to sing there these past few nights. To see if the *cantinero* feels she is worth the gringo Rutledge's price."

"Well?" Lynch said.

Kelso told him.

"Another goddam lie!" Lynch said. "Annie wouldn't agree to nothing like that."

"Hell, it ain't no different than she was doing in Bonner."

"The hell it ain't! She was performing for white men there. And Emory's was a first-class saloon, not a stinking deadfall like one these Mex cantinas."

"And Emory was a first-class citizen, the way I remember it. He wanted to trade you to the Comanches so's to save his saloon," Kelso said. "Well, I believe this buckaroo is telling it straight. At least we'll try to find out for sure. It's something to look into."

Lynch didn't say any more, just glowered at the vaquero as if it was all his fault what had happened to Annie.

Kelso said, "Take the bullets out of his gun and give it back to him."

Lynch did so sullenly.

"Now," Kelso said to the vaquero, "go back to your cattle. Has Rutledge paid for them yet?"

"Si, señor, that he has just done. He has just paid our *jefe* for them." A sly look crossed his face. "You may fight Rutledge, eh?"

"You wouldn't object — now that you are paid, no?"

"I think no, señor."

"Then tell your *compadres* how they gain nothing if they interfere, eh? Explain how they may even profit."

202

The vaquero smiled broadly, and when he did he showed that his teeth had been filed to points, and Kelso knew then he was a Yaqui for sure.

"I will explain it all to them *muy* carefully, señor," he said. "And I hope you get your woman."

The Cantina Flores looked no better nor worse than the other cantinas of the town, although it was on the dirt main street and easily found by Kelso.

He and Lynch had waited until night, resting in the hotel room to avoid running afoul of Mata or other functionaries of the crooked town.

They slipped out quietly past the hotel clerk's blank stare and suppered in the nearest restaurant. Then they made their way to the livery where Kelso had bought a third mount that day after his discussion with the Yaqui vaquero near the cattle holding ground. This one was for Annie. He expected to be moving fast in a few hours.

Now they rode easily up to the cantina and tied to its hitchrack. From within came the sweetly blatant music of a mariachi band.

"Don't do anything foolish when you see her," Kelso said. "If that vaquero was telling it straight — well, let me handle this."

"Seems like you're always in charge," Lynch said. "Nothing new."

Kelso caught the resentment, but ignored it. He had other things on his mind. Lynch's sometimes impulsive behavior was one of them. It struck him again how much Lynch was like a Comanche, like Piavah even, in this respect. This, too, was something he had acquired during those years growing up as their captive, he supposed.

They entered the smoke-filled place and stood searching through the crowd for an empty table, which they found against a far wall. A Mexican girl came to them and they ordered beer. She returned after a while with their drinks and left again. The mariachi band continued to play.

Kelso began to wonder how long they would have to wait.

The place was nearly filled now and still the mariachi went on interminably. Then suddenly the mariachi stopped and a girl appeared on the dais beside them, and she was Annie.

Lynch began to swear in a low voice.

Kelso felt his own shock, even though he had believed what the Yaqui had told him. Annie was dressed in the *chamaca* style, with a short, tight green skirt and a loose white blouse which left bare her shoulders and the tops of her breasts.

She was greeted by whistling and some stomping of feet.

The band played a beginning, and Annie began to sing, a husky contralto that seemed out of place with the accompanying instruments, which themselves were out of place with the gringo tune; yet the whole was pleasing. An unlikely rendition of "Girl in a Gilded Cage," if he'd ever heard one, Kelso thought. But mighty appropriate. And the mixed crowd of gringos and Mexicans loved it.

And then her eyes found them at their table and her voice broke for a moment, before she caught herself and went on with the song. Her glance passed over the crowd, then returned to them, and Kelso thought he could see a beseeching look in her eyes.

She finished the song, then went into another.

Lynch was swearing again, a dull muttering that was like some strange incantation.

Kelso said, "Shut up," and Lynch stopped, then said, "What the hell is going on?"

"She knows we're here."

"I know that. Let's grab her and run."

"With this crowd after us? We'd be lynched by the gringos or stood to the wall by the greasers."

"We came to get her," Lynch said stubbornly.

Kelso said, "Wait." Then, "I didn't know she could sing that well. No wonder Emory was screaming when he lost her in Bonner."

"I told you she was good. But what the hell is she doing singing here? What's that bastard Rutledge got to do with this?"

She ended her singing, took a wild applause, then hurriedly, as if she feared someone would prevent it, she stepped down from the dais and moved to their table and sat down.

"For chrissakes, Annie, what's going on?" Lynch said. "What're you doing in a dive like this?"

Kelso thought he saw tears in her eyes, and he was surprised because he thought she was too tough to cry.

She said, "It's the only way I can get out of that stinking jail they hold me in. I was hoping you'd find me, maybe. Thank God you got here. You don't know what it is to be locked up where nobody but Rutledge and a Rurale named Mata knows where you are."

"Where's Rutledge now?"

"I don't know. Either he or Mata rented me out to Flores, the *cantinero* here, with an option to buy. I'm a slave."

"Did Rutledge beat you?" Kelso said.

"Not on the face. He's no fool. Not where

it shows. Not when I'm merchandise for Flores." She paused. "I got bruises aplenty where it don't show."

"The bastard!" Lynch said.

"I grabbed at the chance to sing here, when he proposed it. It was my only hope — it gave me exposure where you might find me." She looked around the cantina with apprehension and said, "When I've done my stint here, Mata will take me and lock me up again."

"We've got to get you out of here without upsetting the customers," Kelso said.

There were already calls being made in their direction, some of them carrying an ugly tone. The patrons here had come to hear the gringa sing. She was the attraction here, as she had been in Emory's saloon in Bonner — more so even because here she was a novelty among the Mexican girls.

A fat Mexican was coming toward them. Annie said in a low voice, "It's Flores."

Flores came up scowling. He said in English, "Get up and sing, you whore."

"Rough language, friend," Kelso said.

"Do not tell me how to run my business," the *cantinero* said. "She costs me money. You order two *cervezas* and try to tell me how to run my business?"

"Have you bought her yet?" Kelso said. "Have you paid your money for her?"

Startled, Flores said, "Not yet —" and caught himself.

"You are lucky then," Kelso said, and drew his sixgun and held it low at the side of the table, but where Flores could see it was pointed at his belly. "Because we are about to take her with us. If you do not object."

Flores looked at the gun and said, "I do not object."

"Good."

"But there are those here who might." The *cantinero* gestured with his head toward the crowd, which was showing increased impatience although the mariachi band was playing to entertain them.

"That is a problem," Kelso admitted.

"There is a bigger problem," Flores said. "Outside is a Rurale on guard duty. By order of the *jefe*, Mata. Just in case the gringa should take it in her head to leave."

"Then we will all leave together, *cantinero*."

"Very unwise," Flores said.

"Well, we are not the Three Wise Men, are we?" Kelso said. He kept his eyes on Flores but said to Lynch and the girl, "Ready?"

Lynch said, "Yeah."

"Annie?"

"I guess so. Oh, I hope — yes, ready."

"We all stand up and walk out the front door," Kelso said.

"Lead the way, *cantinero*."

"Against my will, señor."

"Of course."

Behind them, without looking, Kelso could feel the bewilderment of the patrons, and knew it would not last long without someone taking action. "*Ándele, ándele,*" he said to Flores. "Go on!"

Flores had sensed the sentiment of the crowd, too, and had hesitated, but now he moved again.

They had almost reached the door when a half-drunk customer, resentful at the interrupting of his entertainment, pulled out a gun and blasted a shot through the ceiling.

The shot brought the Rurale, posted outside, to action. He stepped to the side of the door and drew his pistol as Kelso shoved Flores from behind. Flores grunted as the Rurale's pistol jabbed his belly. "No, no, *hombre!*" he husked at the guard. It was luck that the Rurale did not pull the trigger.

"Back, man, back!" the *cantinero* said, his sweat glistening in the shine of the lantern hung outside the cantina.

Puzzled, the Rurale stepped back, looking at Flores's face.

Lynch slipped past and chopped his own gun down across the Rurale's wrist, knocking his pistol to the ground. He reached down and grabbed it up and shoved it into his belt.

"Stand where you are," Kelso said. "Both of you. Block that door. If you move forward, you're dead."

He moved toward the three horses he'd bought, keeping his eyes on the men in the doorway. Someone inside shoved hard against them, but Flores braced his bulk, sweat running in rivulets down his cheeks.

Kelso waited until Lynch and the girl were mounted, then loosened his own reins and swung into the saddle, still watching the two men bracing against the crowd.

The pressure suddenly pried them loose. They went sprawling, and those behind spilled out like escaping liquid and ran over the two fallen men.

The one in the lead was the one who'd shot through the ceiling. He raised his gun and aimed at Kelso, unsteady with drink, and with a lucky shot Kelso knocked the gun out of his hand. The drunk howled with pain, grabbed his gun hand and bent double in agony.

Kelso pivoted and led the way racing down the street, expecting a fusillade to follow. When it did not, he realized it was because the crowd was afraid of hitting Annie, and this gave him an indication of the esteem in which they held her as an entertainer.

Just ahead, the main street turned at right angles and headed north. They got around the corner and Kelso breathed his relief.

"We made it!" Lynch yelled exultantly.

"Thank God!" Annie said.

And that's when they ran head-on into Rutledge and his men coming down the street. In the poor light of the scattered street lanterns, it was a moment before either recognized the other. When they did both sides halted.

Rutledge's eyes swept the girl and went back to Kelso. He grinned. "You got the pat hand," he said. "Ride by. You're welcome to her."

Kelso felt his nerves honed to a bitter edge as he met Rutledge's stare. All the rage he felt against the man came to a head. For what he'd caused Lynch and himself to go through. And for what he'd done to Annie. Especially Annie. He'd only beat her where it wouldn't show, he thought. Mighty considerate. He wanted to kill the bastard. A wild recklessness took him.

It took Lynch first. Lynch said, "It ain't that simple," and drew his Colt and fired.

In the bad light, and with his eyes on Kelso, Rutledge saw the movement too late. He made his own frantic draw and shot wildly, grazing Annie's horse. The horse reared, spilling her into the street.

Rutledge was hit in the arm and dropped his weapon and it bounced toward Annie.

Lynch swung his aim to the man beside Rutledge and caught him full in the chest. The man's own shot went high as he was driven backward.

Kelso shot the nearest one on the other side, and he fell out of his saddle.

Annie, on her knees, fumbled up Rutledge's fallen gun and raised it.

Then Rutledge did a peculiar thing. He raked his spurs and plunged his horse toward her, bent on trampling her under its hoofs.

In the bar of light from a fronting window, she saw the distortion of his features, the lust to inflict pain, and she knew it for what it was, the final thrust of a man seeking satisfaction of his sadistic needs.

She coldly shot up at him and saw the bullet split the leather of the saddle pommel and the blood spurt through the crotch of his pants. She rolled sidewise clear of the horse and looked after it as Rutledge fell to the street clutching at his groin in one last moment of agony.

"All right," she said. "All right, you sonofabitch! You never quite had it like that before, did you?"

Chapter 15

The two of Rutledge's men still in the saddle made a run for the angle in the street and disappeared around it. Lynch emptied his gun after them and missed.

Kelso had jumped from his saddle to help Annie to her feet. "Are you all right?"

She nodded.

He helped her onto her horse and noticed that she kept her eyes averted from the fallen figure of Rutledge. When he looked closer and saw the nature of the wound that had killed him, he understood why.

"Did you mean to hit him where you did?"

"I told you I could shoot," she said.

"I believe it now." He took a final look back to where the street cornered. There was no sight of the outlaw survivors or of the men who had spilled from the cantina.

Grimly, he figured the fleeing riders had halted the angry crowd. Their flight would make the cantina patrons think twice about further pursuit, even had they been mounted.

As to Rutledge's men he had little concern. Their kind were quick to leave, once they lost a leader. They weren't likely to try to avenge Rutledge's death, either. Their loyalties almost never ran that deep.

Kelso rode fast now, wanting to leave the town behind, wanting to get away from Mata and his squad of Rurales. Because Kelso wasn't at all sure what interest Mata might have in the girl, he said to her, "Where does Mata fit in here?"

She shrugged. "He was only doing a favor for Rutledge, keeping me in the jail. That's what I think, anyway."

"I wouldn't trust that Mata none," Lynch said.

"Who's trusting?" Kelso said. "But what would he want us for?"

"Bastard like that could find a reason. If nothing else because we're Texans and he's Mex."

"Wouldn't likely put himself out for that."

"I wouldn't trust him not to," Lynch said.

"Maybe we done him a favor, killing Rutledge," Kelso said. "It was Mata told us where to find him. He must have had a reason."

Annie said, "Mr. Kelso, how could a Rurale run a town like that? He's supposed to keep the law, ain't he?"

"You find crooks everywhere. You know

that. You ain't that innocent."

Her face reddened and she said hotly, "I never said I was."

"I didn't mean it that way," he said, and knew he was only making it worse. He shut up, angry at himself for hurting her feelings. Or had he? Was she really that sensitive or was she only putting on an act? Hell, he never had understood women.

They had gone six miles, pushing northward as a still-large moon rose to light the landscape, when they heard the sound of gunfire from beyond a cluster of low hills just to their right.

Kelso pulled up, listening, then turned up a draw in the direction of the sound. Lynch fell in behind him and Annie followed. Kelso peered over the brow of the draw and was startled to see a bunch of Indians trapped in a narrow valley by the surrounding fire of hidden riflemen. The riflemen appeared to be shooting from both sides and ahead of the Indians, and to have closed in behind as well. Indians and horses were going down.

It was a slaughter, Kelso thought. As well-staged an ambush as he'd ever heard of.

He was trying to identify the ambushers, many of them partly visible though hid in shadow.

Lynch said suddenly, "Those Injuns are

Comanche. Chrissakes, I think it's Piavah's bunch!"

"Ain't that a picnic?" Kelso said. "Look down there. We got a mix of Mex soldiers and Rurales. Looks like the whole garrison from San Carlos may be in on it."

"What for?"

Kelso pointed back down the valley. "Look back there. A herd of cows the same size as those we seen yesterday at the holding ground. Rutledge's cattle. Them damn Comanches must have stole them in broad daylight and started north with them."

"And Mata picked up their trail?" Lynch said. "Goddam! Ain't that a pretty sight? This is a time I'm rooting for the Mexes."

Piavah appeared to be trying to rally his braves. The surprise had them in complete rout. Whichever way they turned they were in withering fire.

Within minutes the ground was strewn with Comanche casualties.

"Does my heart good!" Lynch said.

But Piavah showed unexpected leadership then. By blowing his bugle, followed by yelled commands, he got some control over the panicked braves, and suddenly those who were still mounted made a concerted charge northward, straight into the fire that blocked them, but out of the crossfire of the trap.

Sheer desperation carried them up to the blockading Mexicans and drove them through to overrun the Mexican position. Mexican soldiers went under, and in a few seconds the wild-riding Comanches were beyond and in the clear and racing up the trail, leaving behind their wounded.

The Mexicans did not pursue them, but instead rushed out of concealment to shoot and club to death those left behind.

"Goddam!" Lynch said again. "Ain't that a beautiful sight?"

The Mexicans gave no quarter. They ran from corpse to corpse to take the Comanche scalps.

"Bad day for Piavah," Kelso said. "What luck he had down in Chihuahua, I don't know. But any he had, he sure lost here. Wasn't more than twenty braves got away."

"Not bad," Lynch said. "Not bad at all, seeing he started off the reservation with near forty."

Kelso had a sobering thought. "That won't be helping his disposition none when he gets back in Texas — if he gets back."

Lynch appeared to be enjoying the sight too much to pay notice.

The soldiers and the Rurales finished their hacking of Comanche corpses and remounted and turned back southward to where a few

217

were holding the cattle bunched. At that distance it was impossible to tell if Mata was among the charro-clad figures, and Kelso figured, anyway, that it was of little concern to him.

The way north to the river was clear, except for the fleeing remnants of Piavah's band, it appeared.

It wouldn't do to overtake Piavah, that was sure, especially after the fearful beating he had just taken. But if they paced themselves carefully —

He waited until the Mexicans he could see were well down the valley toward the herd. Then he said, "Let's hit for Texas," and fell into the trail taken by the Comanches. It was soon apparent that this was one of the main trails north.

They rode steadily for a quarter of an hour, and the smell of dust ahead decreased gradually so that they knew the Comanches were keeping a faster pace and pulling farther ahead of them with every mile. That was what they wanted. Let the Kwahadies increase their lead.

Kelso's mind was on this when he heard Annie call out to him. He turned in his saddle and saw her pointing behind them and saw a half-dozen Rurales coming up fast.

Lynch saw them, too, and said, "We going to run for it?"

"Where to? Piavah's bunch is up ahead."

Lynch said, "I don't trust that bastard Mata none."

The Rurales kept coming, and Kelso saw that it was Mata who was leading them.

A Rurale waved a hand in a friendly gesture, and Kelso reined up, unsure, thinking that Lynch was probably right. By then it was too late.

Sergeant Mata came up smiling. "*Hola, ranger!*" he said.

And still smiling he, along with his men, whipped out his revolver and held it steady. "Too bad for you, Tejano, that I dropped my prized carbine during the fight back there, and came with my men to look for it. You were just disappearing into the haze."

Kelso knew then he had made a mistake, but he said, "Too bad? Why?"

"Because I see you have the girl, and I have decided she belongs to me. Your friend Rutledge may dispute this, but that is no concern of yours."

"Rutledge is dead."

Mata looked surprised, then smiled again. "Good. You killed him, eh, ranger?"

Annie said, "I killed him."

"So?" Mata looked at her with appraisal. "It is a hard thing to believe. Did you shoot him in the back?"

Annie looked at him with hate in her eyes.

"I shot him in the balls," she said.

Mata blinked. For a long moment he did not speak. Then he said, "That is a thing to remember." He paused. "Well, now you will come with me. And I will see you do not have a gun."

Kelso had had enough. All the frustration of these past weeks, all the resentment of the unwanted assignment which had got him involved in an impossible relationship with Lynch and the girl, boiled over. For one wild second he was about to grab for his gun.

And that's when a couple of Comanches shot from the rocks above them and knocked two Rurales out of their saddles.

Mata's eyes swept the valley slope and spotted the fire flashes as the Indians fired again. He seemed to forget the gringos he was holding under the gun and drove his spurs in and went charging up the slope, the other Rurales at his heels.

The Comanches fired again and missed, and then the Rurales were upon them, sixguns blazing at close quarters. The Indians went down.

"Come on!" Kelso shouted, and started up the main trail at a dead run, Annie and Lynch instantly following.

They could hear the yells of the Rurales and then the singing of short rounds ricocheting off the rocky terrain around them.

There was a turn here and they made it and were for the moment out of sight and range. They drove the horses hard, but they could hear the Rurales coming onto the trail and pounding up it, and they remembered the wild recklessness of their charge against the two Comanches. It wasn't something to make Kelso's mind easy. If he had counted right, there were still four Rurales back there, including Mata.

The low hills flattened out, and they rode through chaparral and cactus, which hid the back trail from Kelso's sight. But out of sight wasn't out of mind; he knew Mata was back there somewhere.

He kept pushing the horses until they reached the river, and then he pushed them across the brownish water, which moved sluggishly here over the sand shallows of the ford. Off to the southeast, the current quickened as the river fell away into a gorge. For a moment he debated whether to turn down that way to get off the trail, but he decided against it.

He allowed a brief halt to let the horses and themselves drink hurriedly, and to scoop full the canteens they carried.

Annie said, "Will they cross the river, Mr. Kelso?"

"Why not?"

"But Rurales aren't allowed into Texas."

"Rangers aren't allowed into Mexico, either," Kelso said. He rode into the fringe of tule reeds and turned for another look across the water. He saw nothing and turned back to the trail, wondering hopefully if the Rurales had given up the chase after all.

There was no real reason Mata should continue. He didn't have to have Annie. There were plenty of Mexican girls in San Carlos, and Mata did not seem like a man who'd center his desire on a particular one. Not to the extent of risking a bushwhacking.

Just as he had himself nearly convinced of this, he heard the slap of a bullet against the water and heard the crack of a carbine from the brush on the other side of the Rio.

Well, there went his hope. Mata had given his answer. He was out to get a Texas Ranger, Kelso thought. Kelso's escape was a personal affront to him; it would goad him much deeper than losing a saloon girl, for whatever she was worth to him.

He remembered back again to that time at Guadalupe and knew that Mata had been nursing this grudge ever since he'd recognized Kelso in the San Carlos cantina. He'd only waited to satisfy it until he'd seen what Kelso would do against Cole Rutledge.

Firing that wild shot into the tules had been

a damn fool thing to do. It gave Kelso warning. He'd bet Mata was giving some Rurale hell for firing it.

"Now we know," Lynch said, as if reading his mind. "That bastard ain't stopping at the river."

"Oh, my God!" Annie said. "Is it ever going to end?"

As if in answer, a volley of shots zinged by, clipping the stalks around them. It drove them out of the reeds and onto the trail, which wound ahead through barren gullies and washes, scattered great rocks and, five or six hundred yards beyond, up the sloping side of a low mesa.

They rode at a gallop, Annie ahead, Lynch next, Kelso dropping back slightly, his carbine in his hand, although he knew the futility of shooting from horseback at that pace. He let go the reins, though, and twisted in the saddle and let go two fast shots by way of discouragement. They had their effect as he saw the Rurales break out of the screening of tules, then pivot back in, momentarily hesitant.

Their hesitation didn't last. A moment later they were in the open and running hard, knowing there was little danger from Kelso's snap shots.

The Rurales fired, too, but their aim could be little better at that riding gait.

And then they were urging their faltering horses up the climbing trail, with the mesa top close ahead but not close enough, and the Rurales gaining as they still rode the flat ground, and the bullets coming nearer.

Kelso glanced back and saw Mata in the lead, and he could have sworn that Mata was grinning at him.

He looked ahead again, heard a rifle crack and saw Annie slump forward, blood spray staining her white blouse just above the cantle.

Oh, Christ! he thought, she took a bullet!

She straightened then, and he saw the bleeding gash on her horse's rump and felt his relief now that he knew where the blood had come from.

They went up and over the low summit, and the mesa top spread before them with the trail like a highway across it.

"Stop!" Kelso yelled.

They halted and sat their blowing, frothing horses, and Kelso said, "This is as good as any."

They got down and lay sweating behind a strew of rocks that rimmed the way here, waiting for Mata and his Rurales to come up the trail.

But now the trail was empty.

"He's took to the brush," Lynch said. "Thick as it is on them slopes, we'll never spot them. We'd best ride on."

"Not much cover on this mesa."

"Let's ride, dammit!"

"Wait." Kelso looked over at Annie, and she had her gun ready, the one she'd shot Rutledge with. He said, "Seems like every stud in the Southwest has got his eye on you, girl."

She said, "Not Mata, Mr. Kelso. Mata is a one-nighter, if I'm any judge. He don't give a damn about getting me. What he wants is to kill you. I heard him saying so to Cole. Some old set-to, you had."

Kelso nodded. "Yeah. My way of joking, girl."

"Thanks for the compliment," Annie said.

The way she said it, Kelso wasn't sure just what she meant. Had he said something wrong?

He caught a glimpse of a sombrero in the chaparral and let go a quick shot and was surprised when the hat flew up and back, caught by its chin string. He cursed his high shot. You couldn't cut the odds by putting holes in sombreros.

The Rurales now slipped into the shallow arroyos which wrinkled the slope on either side of the trail, and were thus hidden so that neither Kelso nor Lynch could tell how close they were.

But the last fifty yards smoothed out, and

Kelso knew the Rurales couldn't cross this part without partly exposing themselves. The trouble was, there was partial cover even here, and if Mata and his men once reached the rim, Kelso and party would be overwhelmed.

And Mata was just the kind of *machón* who would sacrifice his men, even himself, to satisfy his grudge. His men would do likewise. Kelso had heard of damn few Rurales who lacked guts.

He caught a movement on the slope to his left and studied it, every visible rock and leaf, trying to see a target.

Suddenly a rabbit bounded out of a clump of mesquite which overhung an arroyo, and Kelso put a fast shot into the clump.

A Rurale jumped to his feet, then toppled sideways into the ravine. The way Kelso figured it, there were three Rurales left. And one of them was Mata.

Now a scud of cloud drifted across the sky and blotted out the moon and seemed to hang there, and they could no longer see anything on the slope.

There was a good chance they could be flanked by the Rurales in the darkness. Kelso said, "Mount up. We'll move on out."

Lynch did not object. Waiting there in the dark with the moonlight gone was making all of them nervous.

The trail was easy enough to follow on the mesa; the stars gave enough light for that. They were halfway across it when the cloud moved on and the moon shone again and left them exposed. Kelso looked back, but he could see no sign of the Mexicans.

"Maybe they gave up," Lynch said.

"Maybe."

"It don't make sense they should keep following. They only lost more men by doing it."

"That's what worries me."

"Why?"

"Mata is a *machón*. That's to say he's *muy* macho, or thinks he is," Kelso said. "A real he-man. We've hurt his pride, and pride is what a *machón* lives on. I don't think he'll ever give up now."

"Mr. Kelso," Annie said, "are we going to ride all night?" She sounded wrung out and exhausted.

Kelso thought about this, then said, "No. This mesa top is open enough to see anybody crossing it. We'll fort up on that little butte up ahead and get some rest. But we'll have to watch so they don't sneak up on us."

"And then what?" Lynch said.

Kelso shrugged. "We'll play it like it's dealt."

The butte sloped up a scant thirty feet from

the mesa, an isolated squat cone with a top dished by erosion into a lopsided shallow bowl. The bowl offered a fair amount of protection for them and the horses.

"Spread out around the rim," Kelso said. "We got to watch all directions. Sam, you take that southwest corner. I'll stay here."

Annie said, "What about me?"

"Take the north side, halfway between us."

"It isn't likely they'd come that direction, Mr. Kelso."

"You don't know that," Kelso said. "And neither do I."

"Just so you know I can see as good as either of you."

"Sure, sure," he said.

"And shoot, too. And I'll stay awake."

"I said sure, didn't I?"

"Just so you don't forget."

"I won't."

He was damn sure none of them would fall asleep, not with Mata and his two remaining Rurales out there figuring to kill them. But two hours passed without them seeing any movement on the nearly bare plateau.

Kelso began to wonder if either of the others had dozed off in spite of the danger, but he was afraid to call to them. He didn't want to risk giving away their position, if by chance Mata didn't know it. And he was likewise afraid to leave his own lookout spot for fear of missing something.

He worried mostly about Annie. She had been through a lot these last few days, and in the moonlit quiet she might have succumbed to sleep despite her determination not to. He was tempted to make a quick inspection to check on her.

And then she was suddenly at his elbow. "Mr. Kelso?"

"Yeah!" He was startled. "What the hell are you doing here?"

"You going to get us out of this alive?"

"Sure."

"Are you sure?"

"Sure."

"I don't know how you can be so sure."

"I am, that's all." Her hand was on his arm now, moving as if in caress. He felt it that way, and he felt a warm flush in his groin. "You don't have to call me *mister*," he said.

"Can you see Sam? Is he over there?" Annie asked.

"He's over there. I can see him. And he can see us, too, if he's looking this way."

There was a silence, then she said, "Too bad. I owe you a lot — I'd be willing to show my appreciation."

"Goddammit!" he said. Then, "No. Not now, for chrissakes! You forgetting Mata is out there? And Sam over there, he'd shoot the both of us." He was breathing so heavy he almost choked on the words.

"Can he see us?"

"Of course he can see! I told you that."

"Too bad," she said again. "Well, anyway, I wanted you to know how I felt."

He groaned. And suddenly Lynch's voice called out, a dead giveaway to Mata. "What's going on over there?" Lynch's boots came stomping across the bowl, moving fast.

Annie slipped away toward her own post, leaving Kelso alone to face him.

Lynch said, "Whose idea was that?"

"What idea?"

"You two cosying up like that."

"Cosying? There wasn't any cosying, Sam."

"The hell there wasn't. She came to you, didn't she? I knew it was going to happen. You keep on making out the hero in front of her and it was bound to be."

"I don't know what you're talking about."

"You know, all right."

"It ain't my fault how she feels. I've only been doing what had to be done. You know that," Kelso said. In spite of his own feelings for the girl, he felt sorry for Lynch.

Lynch stood there gripping his carbine, his face unnaturally white in the moonlight, his eyes shadowed into black-filled sockets like

230

those of a skull. A death's head if Kelso had ever seen one. Kelso felt his skin crawl.

He said, "Sam, don't do nothing foolish. And get to hell back on guard!"

Lynch began to swear, and kept it up for a long time. Then, abruptly, he stopped and stood silent for a moment before he turned away and stalked over toward his own lookout.

Kelso swore too, then. Partly in relief, and partly as he realized they had given Mata and his Rurales a damned good chance to close in on them. He hurried to scan the mesa.

A carbine cracked and a bullet whined off a boulder, just beside his head. He whirled about, his own weapon coming up. He almost blasted Lynch before he saw Lynch was just now turning at the sound of the ricochet.

It wasn't Lynch, it was Mata. He turned back, went prone on the basin rim, searching out the sparse growth for some hiding place of the Rurales. There didn't appear to be enough cover out there to hide a jackrabbit, let alone three Mexicans in big sombreros.

And abruptly, Annie was back. "Are you all right?" she said. She lay dawn alongside him as he kept looking for the Rurales.

"Get back to your watch," he said, and shoved at her with one hand, the other grasping his carbine. When she didn't move, he let his hand linger.

She said softly, "Any time you want, Mr. Kelso."

His voice was hoarse when he answered. "Not now, for chrissakes!" He wondered if the danger was exciting her.

She gave a nervous laugh. "Sorry. I just wanted you to keep it in mind."

He said tightly, "I got it in mind, girl. You can believe that!"

And then he saw them. Off to the east there was a roll in the plateau, visible now only because the changing position of the moon had thrown the defile into shadow. It was, Kelso judged, a hundred yards away. And on its near rim he glimpsed the glint of a rifle barrel being withdrawn. Then it reappeared, belched smoke that sent a bullet whipping past his ear as he rose slightly for a better sight. He jerked back down.

"What will they do now?" Annie said.

"I don't know. They still got three against two of us."

"Two?" she said. "Two?" She slapped the pistol she was holding. "Not two, Mr. Kelso. Three. I've got this."

"I was forgetting."

"That was no accident with Cole Rutledge. I hit him where I was aiming."

"I believe you," he said.

Lynch came scrambling toward them and

said, "Nothing on the other side that I can see."

"Get the hell back there, anyway," Kelso said. "How many times do I have to tell you?"

Lynch did not move for a long, strained moment. Then he turned without a word and left.

"He's jealous, Mr. Kelso."

"Hell, I know that."

There was no sight of the Rurales now, no more shots fired from the gully.

"They're up to something," Kelso said. He kept running his eyes over the terrain with its shadows seeming to ever change.

Then suddenly he could see them coming, could see them ride up out of the wash, spurring their horses to a run, kicking up a cloud of dust which made them uncertain targets.

He and Annie both opened fire, and neither hit anything, and then the targets were no longer there at all, were gone as if the ground had swallowed them.

He inched forward on his belly and stared down the side of the butte, and he could see why. There was another gully just below, a ravine actually, with a sharply cut bank formed by storm runoff from the butte itself.

The ravine ran a snakelike course back to the wider wash, and if the Rurales had realized it, they could have sneaked close unnoticed instead of making their reckless charge. Which told Kelso something of their temper, of their prideful guts.

Well, they knew about it now, he thought. And they were hid down there in one of the sharp turns of the ravine. He could expect they would be a little less reckless next time, although you never knew about the macho sonsofbitches.

No, you sure as hell never did. Because even while he was thinking this, they made their charge on foot, appearing from nowhere.

He and Annie thrust their weapons forward to meet the assault, and a chance shot by an attacker struck a stone and sent it slamming against Annie's trigger hand. She dropped her gun, and it fell over the brow and deep into a cleft between two rocks.

Kelso heard it fall and thought she was hit. He jerked his head to look and missed firing before the Rurales gained concealment behind an outcrop of limestone directly below him.

He said, "Holler for Sam," and turned his gaze back down to where the attackers were.

He heard her yell, but Lynch didn't answer. She said, "I don't see him — I'll go look." He heard the loose gravel rolling as she scrambled down into the bowl.

Now he was alone, and here they came again, the three of them leaping up at the same time, only spread out a half-dozen yards apart so he could only get off a shot at one of them.

He picked the one he thought was Mata and sent a bullet into his chest and saw him roll off the butte side clear down to the base as the other two dove into closer cover.

He could see the dead one's face then, lying open to the sky, and knew he'd made a mistake — it wasn't Mata.

Where the hell was Lynch? He had a sudden suspicion that Lynch was staying away deliberately. What better way to eliminate a rival? The damn fool, he thought, he'll get himself killed, too, and Annie taken.

And now he was facing alone the two Rurales, who were hidden so close beneath him that he would not see their next move unless he crawled into the open over the butte's edge.

He glanced behind him and saw no sight of either Lynch or Annie. He swore and turned back to wait for the next assault.

This time only one of them arose, far to the left of where Kelso had expected. He swung his carbine but the man was gone before he could get a shot at him. As he swung back, he saw loosened small rocks avalanching down the slope, indicating that the other, who could be Mata, had moved farther to his right. And all at once he knew what their strategy was.

They would come at him from either side and catch him in their crossfire. He might get one but the other would get him.

Behind him he heard Annie call out, but he couldn't catch her words. Then he glimpsed the Rurale on the left come over the top shooting, and he swung fast and snapped a shot and saw the man go over backwards.

He swung right, and there was Mata with his pistol leveled ten yards away and his teeth showing white with anticipation.

Kelso panicked and squeezed his trigger too quick and knew he would miss. It made no difference because his carbine did not fire, and Mata's teeth were all that was left between Kelso and death.

And then Mata's teeth came out, and his whole grinning face burst into a dark blossom as he took a .45 bullet through the back of his head from Lynch, who had risen just behind him.

Chapter 16

They lived on small game until they were just south of the Pecos, and hunger was always with them. And then they blundered onto a stray longhorn steer which had come from God knows where, and they had their first real meal since they had left San Carlos. They cooked what meat they could carry and pushed on.

And now, with their bellies full, their minds could turn to other things. And that's when the trouble began between them.

Lynch started it; it was a thing that had been growing on him ever since he had found Kelso lying next to Annie back there on the mesa butte.

He started it not by saying anything, just by the suspicious looks he kept giving them. If the looks bothered Annie, she didn't show it. She had a pretty good poker face for a woman, Kelso thought.

But after a while, after he'd caught the covert, angry look of Lynch's eyes on him for a couple of days, and after he'd put up with a silence between them broken only by words of necessity, Kelso got fed up with it.

"You got something eating you?"

"Plenty," Lynch said.

"Get it off your chest."

"You and her," Lynch said, and jerked his head toward Annie, who was riding on the far side of Kelso, away from Lynch.

"What about us?"

"You know damn well, what about."

"Like I said, get it off your chest."

"I know how it is between you."

Kelso rode in silence for a while. Then he said, "These things happen, Sam." He could tell that Annie was listening to what they said.

"That don't make it any easier to know."

"I guess not," Kelso said, and meant it. "But there it is."

Lynch said slowly, "What I owe you, it's a hell of a lot. But there's a limit, maybe, to what it'll cover."

"I ain't asking for your gratitude. Anybody hacked up like you were by them Comanches, I'd probably done the same for. Part of my job."

"You and her," Lynch said, "that part of your job, too?"

"Damn fool question."

"You knew from the start how it was between me and her," Lynch said. "Why'd you have to butt in?"

"Wasn't none of it intentional."

"That don't help."

Kelso turned his head to glance at Annie, and he could see the excitement showing through despite her struggle for self-control. Just like a woman, he thought. Every goddam woman is like that, they can't help themselves. They got a built-in pleasure at seeing men fighting over them.

He said, "So what do you want me to do about it?"

"Stay away from her."

"Sam, you're going to be held by the law for a while, at the very least. You think men are going to stay away from her? Dammit, man, she works in a saloon. You forgetting that?"

"I ain't worried about other men," Lynch said. "They don't mean nothing to her, except she coaxes them into buying drinks. It's you and her I'm worried about. I can see that's something different. I ain't blind."

"Tell *her* that."

"She can hear me, can't she? But it's you I'm telling. Keep your goddam hands off her."

"I ain't had them on her."

"You been coming mighty close."

Annie spoke up. She said, "You don't own me, Sam."

"I want to. I asked you to be my wife. We had something good between us. He's trying to spoil it all."

"I ain't trying to spoil nothing," Kelso said. By God, that was the truth, too. It was just that he couldn't help himself anymore. Ever since that night on the butte, her words kept running through his brain. *Any time you want, Mr. Kelso. I just want you to keep it in mind.*

And his own, *I got it in mind, girl. You can believe that.*

That was for damn sure.

"We got a ways to ride yet, Sam," he said. "Let's drop the subject until we get to Bonner, at least. We got other things to think about."

"You keep your damn hands off her, maybe we can."

"I told you, I ain't touched her."

"Keep your damn mind off her, too."

That, now, was going to be hard to do, but Kelso said, "All right, Sam. It'll be the way you want it." He looked again at Annie, and it seemed to him that she was showing disappointment now. He didn't know if it was because the argument was over, or because of what he'd agreed to. It only brought home to him again that he never had understood women very well. And he sure didn't

240

understand this one.

But looking at the sultry pout of her lips, he wasn't at all sure he was going to live up to the promise he'd made Lynch, anyway. Mind or hands, either, it was going to be damn hard to do.

They rode along without speaking for many miles, and Kelso thought there was an end to it. Then, suddenly, Lynch started it all over again.

He did it by abruptly ordering Annie to come over and ride next to him.

If he had asked, she most likely would have complied. But his tone was rough, and Kelso could sense her stiffening at the demand. She made no move to change her position.

"You hear me?" Lynch said.

"I heard you."

"Well?"

"Maybe I like it where I am."

"Yeah," he said, "I figured that. It's as much your fault as it is his."

"What is?"

"You been throwing yourself at him, that's what."

Kelso said, "Easy what you're saying, Sam."

"Ain't it so?"

When Kelso didn't answer, Lynch went on to Annie, "What's he got to offer you? A Texas Ranger don't get paid enough to support a wife, so he damn sure ain't going to marry you."

Kelso couldn't argue that point, he thought.

Lynch said, "You hear what I'm saying, Annie? He ain't going to marry you."

"Nobody's asking him to. Besides, what business is it of yours?"

"It's all my business, you know that. You know how I feel about you."

"For God's sake, Sam," she said. "Get off it, will you?"

He shut up then, his handsome face taking on a deep hurt before it hardened into grimness.

Looking over at him she saw this, and after riding a few paces, she dropped behind Kelso and swung over to the far side of Sam and drew up beside him. "We're still friends, Sam," she said.

"That ain't enough for me."

"You don't make it any easier."

"I don't want to," he said. "I want you to remember how I feel."

"Sam," she said, "you don't know anything, do you?"

"I know I want you."

"Oh, Christ!" she said.

Kelso was listening to it all, and in spite of his own lust, he felt his old sympathy for Lynch. Being a captive of the Comanches all those years must have really warped his judgment. He just couldn't seem to understand what the girl's feeling toward him had always been, and he couldn't see that he was in deep trouble with the law for killing Indians.

One thing you could say for him, he didn't give up easy. He didn't have a chance in hell, but he didn't give up hope.

And once again Kelso cussed the situation he found himself in, cussed the order given him to bring Lynch in, and cussed all the rest that followed — except the girl. He didn't cuss her.

He began to wonder why he'd become a Ranger in the first place. Well, he had an answer for that. He'd been out of a job and there had been an enlistment opening.

Then, as the years passed, you got in a rut and stayed with what you were doing, which was what most people did. Lynch was an exception there, he had to hand it to him. Lynch had the ambition to bust out of a wrangler's job and strike off on his own. He'd made a mistake picking the spot he did for his horse ranch, or maybe he'd just been unlucky, but at least he'd made a try for a better life. That was more than he, Kelso, had ever done. It made Kelso uneasy, thinking about that.

Why should a man with Lynch's guts and

ambition and desire to make a life for himself — yes, even take a wife — why should he have it all destroyed for him because some goddam Comanche went bronco? And just because Kelso was mindlessly doing a job he'd been instructed to do, doing it against his own will. He wondered then if Lynch, despite his word, would try to escape his custody. Kelso figured he might. But not until they got Annie back to Bonner.

And now, after these several days, the healing wound in Lynch's leg suddenly took on infection. It struck him hard. He got up in the morning and was unable to mount his horse. Annie felt his face and it was burning with fever.

"Can you ride?" Kelso said. "If I get you into the saddle —"

"You go ahead," Lynch said. "Leave me lay. I get feeling better, I'll follow. I ain't up to pounding leather now. I feel like a fly lighting on me would puncture my skin."

"We'll all wait then. Reckon we could use the rest."

"Suit yourself. Just leave me alone. When I'm sick I don't want nobody bothering me."

"Sam," Kelso said, "you're like a damn coyote. A sick coyote acts that way."

"Just get me in the shade of that scrub over

there and leave me be. This fever passes, I'll be all right."

"If that's the way you want it."

They made him as comfortable as they could and put a canteen next to him. And then they moved off several yards until there was a screen of brush between them.

Annie said, "You think he'll be all right?"

Kelso shrugged. "Never know about a fever." He was silent, then said, "But he's lived through a hell of a lot worse."

"We might as well make ourselves comfortable," she said. "I'll look in on him now and then."

"Sure," he said.

They sprawled out, relishing the chance to rest from the hard pace of these past couple of weeks. A lot had happened, it had taken its toll.

He lay there relaxed, with Annie only a few feet away, and he felt his juices taking hold. He thought of Lynch over there suffering, and it bothered him the way his thoughts were working. It bothered him, but not enough and not for long. He got up and moved over to lie beside her.

Neither spoke at first, then Annie reached out a hand and touched him. She said, "You thinking about that night on the butte, Mr. Kelso?"

"Somewhat."

"What I said then — it goes."

"You make it damn hard for me," he said.

"I'm trying to make it easy."

"Too damn easy," he said huskily. He rolled over and pulled her breasts against him and pressed his mouth on hers with a fierce hunger. "I ain't had a woman in a long time," he said.

"I'm here," she said. "And I owe you."

"That's all it is?"

"Do you care?"

He squeezed her. "Reckon I don't."

"Well, then," she said.

A long time later he lay beside her staring at the sky. He could tell by the rhythm of her breathing that she was replete and drowsy herself. It had gone well, he thought. For the first time in a long time he felt at peace with the world.

Lynch's voice came from close by, jerking him erect. His eyes searched wildly. And there Lynch was, delirious with fever, a crazy look on his face, a gun in his hand and pointed at Kelso.

"You sonofabitch!" Lynch said.

"Easy, Sam. Listen to me. You got a fever, Sam."

Lynch stared at him as if he wasn't there. "Get away from my wife," he said. His words were bit off and heavy with threat. His tone was sane, in contrast to his look, and that chilled Kelso worst of all.

"Now wait a minute, Sam —"

"You had to have her, didn't you?"

"I don't know what you're talking about."

"Hell," Lynch said, "I was watching. I seen it all."

Kelso heard Annie's quick-drawn breath.

"I was watching all the time," Lynch said.

"Watching what, Sam?"

"I seen you making love to her."

"You're out of your head, Sam. With a fever. You got to listen to me when I tell you that. You got a fever because your leg is infected, and it makes you imagine things."

"I seen it."

"You think you seen it. It's just the fever. I ain't ever lied to you, have I, Sam?"

Lynch seemed to be trying to think. The gun he was holding sagged. Finally he said, "Maybe I was seeing things."

Annie said, "You shouldn't be up and around, Sam. You ought to be resting."

"Yeah. Maybe you're right. I don't feel good."

"You go back and lay down," Kelso said. "It's the best thing for you."

"Yeah. I must have been dreaming." Lynch looked from one to the other of them, seemed to lose his thought. He turned and staggered back to where his blanket was.

Kelso blew out his breath.

Annie giggled, nervous with relief.

"I ain't sure it was worth that," he said. "He looked crazy as hell. Especially with that gun pointed at me."

"A hell of a thing to tell a girl."

"Yeah. Well, I guess it was worth the scare. But not if he'd pulled the trigger."

"Gives you something to think about, don't it, Mr. Kelso?"

"Sure as hell does."

She laughed again, this time with amusement.

She stopped abruptly as they heard the sound of wood splintering from over where Lynch had gone.

Kelso jumped up and ran cursing toward him.

Lynch had Kelso's carbine grasped by the barrel and was standing dazedly next to a boulder against which he had just smashed the weapon's stock. He appeared as if he did not know what he had done.

Kelso snatched the carbine from him and then groaned. It was still usable, but he'd hate to rely on its accuracy. He had a sudden urge to smash the barrel, too, only over Lynch's head.

The impulse went as Lynch, weakened from his efforts, collapsed into a heap.

The next day Lynch's fever was gone and his wound seemed less swollen. His head was clear and he was stubborn as ever. "Let's go. I'm ready to ride," he said. He made no mention of the incident of the previous day.

Chapter 17

They were into the Panhandle now, and that is where they saw the first example of Piavah's vented rage, the first of his bitter retaliation for his defeated Moon Raid: the remains of a burned-out ranch and a strew of four mutilated bodies in the fore yard. They stopped long enough to bury the dead, then moved on, hoping not to see what they feared they would see.

Ten miles farther on they saw it; this time the victim was a lone man. A single shack had been all he'd had — barely a start, Kelso thought. He'd never had a chance. They buried him, too.

And again, twenty miles beyond and within a dozen miles of Lynch's old place, they found the third. A young man and his wife, terribly hacked, their neatly laid-out ranch razed to a black stubble.

Lynch said nothing. Kelso said, "Like your place, last year."

"Oh, God!" Annie said. After a single glance

she no longer looked at the bodies or the ruins. Instead she stared off into the distance while the men again performed their graveside task.

"He's taking his revenge now — for everything," Kelso said.

"Their name was Hanford," Lynch said. "Charley Hanford. I knew them slightly. They had a kid, a boy maybe eight years old." He paused. "They must have taken the kid."

They finished their job and remounted, and with Annie between them, sobbing softly, they were riding away when Kelso heard the sound in the brush. He had his gun in his hand without thinking, and said in a low voice, "There's something in there."

"Comanch?" Lynch said. "Wounded, maybe. Let's get the bastard." His own gun was out, and he was about to fire blindly at where they again heard a faint whimper, as of pain.

"Hold on!" Kelso said. "Goddammit, don't take no brush shots."

Lynch scowled, but held his fire.

Kelso suddenly rode recklessly into the brush and came out on the other side with a small figure running before him.

Lynch said tightly, "It's the Hanford kid."

And Annie said in a choked voice, "You almost shot him."

Kelso caught up to the kid, leaned from

the saddle and grabbed him. "Hold on, boy!"

The Hanford kid stopped and looked up with a face filled with hate. The hate faded as he took in Kelso's range clothes. He looked even younger than eight. Kelso climbed down to stand in front of him, and did not know what to say.

Behind him Annie slipped from her horse and went to the boy and put her arms around him. She pulled his head against her breasts and said, "It's all right. It's all right, honey."

The boy had a shock of black hair and skin darkened from the sun. He wasn't crying. He said, "The Injuns killed my ma and pa."

Annie said softly, "We know."

"Someday I'll kill them back," the boy said.

"Oh, God," Annie said, and held him tight.

"Let him ride with you," Kelso said to her. Then to the boy, "We buried your folks, son."

"I know," the boy said. "I watched."

Lynch said, "If you watched, why didn't you come out from being hid?"

"I was scared," the boy said. "Scared the Comanches would come back."

Lynch nodded. "Reckon I know how you feel, kid. I once felt the same way. A long time ago." He was thinking back, then said, "Name is Zack, ain't it?"

"Yes, sir," the boy said. "Zachary Hanford."

"All right, Zack," Kelso said. "You mount up behind the lady there. You got any other folks around here?"

"No, sir."

Kelso looked at Annie. She met his glance and seemed to know what he was thinking. She said, "We're going to Bonner, aren't we?"

"Yeah." He hesitated. "Might be somebody there can look after him."

Her chin lifted and she said, "There is."

He gave her a long, steady glance, then without another word he turned and led off.

"Thank God, them Comanch didn't find him," Lynch said. "I'd hate for him to go through what I went through as a kid."

"He's been through a part of it."

"Not the worst part," Lynch said. "Not by a damn sight."

Kelso said, "Looks like what we feared would happen is happening."

Lynch said tightly, "You mean Piavah?"

"Looks like he's torching the whole damn Panhandle, don't it?"

"And you're blaming me."

Kelso didn't answer directly. Instead, he said, "Maybe if he'd made a successful raid down there in Mexico he'd have gone back on the reservation and forgotten the rest."

"Well, he didn't."

"No telling when he'll stop."

"They'll send the cavalry in now, won't they?" Annie said.

Kelso said, "Of course. But a lot of settlers could die before the Army catches up with him. He'll get what he wants, I reckon — to be known as the last Comanche war chief."

The boy, riding behind Annie, said again, "They killed my ma and pa. Did you know that?"

"Try not to think about it," Annie said. She reached a hand around in back to touch him.

"I'll always think about it," the boy said. "I ain't ever going to forget what they done."

Lynch said to Kelso, "If they'd took the kid, they'd have turned him into a true Comanche most likely, young as he is. He'd forget, maybe. What they done with me, it was a little different. I was a couple years older."

"If they took him back to the reservation, he might be recognized as white."

"It ain't likely. Not with that black hair and dark skin. Ain't as if he was a blue-eyed blond and would stand out in a crowd of Injuns. Hell, he'd blend right in. You got to remember the Comanches got a lot of part-breeds mixed in, mostly Mex but some got gringa blood. Been a lot of white women taken over the years that you never hear about. Comanch women have a low birth rate, and the bucks raise most part-breed bastards just like their own. No, if they'd took the Hanford kid, it ain't likely anybody'd ever pick him out." He paused, then said, "I'd rather see the boy dead than raised to be a Comanche."

"I guess I know your feelings."

Lynch looked back at Annie, riding with the boy behind her. "Too bad I got to go in for trial," he said. "Me and Annie could adopt the boy, maybe."

Kelso shook his head slightly. It looked to him like Lynch was never going to give up. No matter what she said or how she treated him, he wasn't ever going to believe she wouldn't come back.

Lynch dropped back to ride beside her and the boy. He said, "You know that Kelso is taking me in."

She looked at him with pained sympathy and said softly, "I know, Sam. I'm sorry."

"If I get a Texan jury, I'll likely get off."

"I hope so, Sam."

"What I'm thinking is — I mean, while I'm standing trial — well, maybe you could look after the boy some."

"I intend to."

"Then when I come back we could raise him together."

"Please, Sam —"

"Hell, no jury made up of Texans is going

to find a man guilty for killing Comanches. Be like condemning him for killing rattlers."

"That isn't what I mean. Oh, I don't know what I mean!"

"It'll be all right, Annie. You'll see."

The boy said, "Mister, I'm going to kill them Comanches that killed my ma and pa."

"I know how you feel, Zack."

"You'll see," the boy said.

"He doesn't cry," Annie said to Lynch.

"His hate is keeping him from it," Lynch said. "I know that hate."

"He's only a child, Sam. Eight years old."

"He's old enough to hate." Lynch said to the boy, "You hate them red sonofabitches, don't you, kid?"

The boy nodded. "Red sonofabitches!"

"Sam!"

"Just showing you," Lynch said. "That's why he don't cry. Maybe he'll cry tomorrow or the next day. But not now. He's too full of hate."

Lynch took off his hat to wipe the sweat from his brow, and the Hanford kid stared at him, then said, "You been scalped, mister?"

Lynch put his hat back on quickly. "Yeah, kid."

"Maybe you can help me kill them red sonofabitches," the boy said.

"Sure, kid. Maybe I can."

Annie said, "You think we may run into them?"

"Don't see any sign. When they left the Hanford place, their tracks went due east."

"They might turn north, though."

"No telling. I hope not. Not with you and the kid with us."

"I couldn't take any more of them, Sam. I couldn't stand any more."

"Well, they headed east. I don't know what for. Looking for another ranch to burn, more whites to kill."

The Hanford kid said suddenly, "Mister, are you the man that scalped them Comanches up on the reservation?"

Lynch exchanged glances with Annie, then said, "Yeah, kid. That was me."

The boy said, "My pa, he said it was your fault the Comanches were on the warpath. He said that. Said it just a few days before they come and killed him and ma. My pa said you made the Injuns mad and now they'd come and kill all the white people in the Panhandle." After a pause, he said, "My pa was right, wasn't he?"

Lynch didn't answer him. Instead, he kicked at his horse and moved up to ride beside Kelso.

Kelso had heard the conversation between Lynch and the boy, and he wasn't surprised at the way Lynch was taking it. It would be a hell of a thing to have on your conscience, he thought, although he wasn't at all sure how much responsibility Lynch felt for what was happening. The man had his own way of looking at things.

They approached Bonner and entered the town, and Kelso noted there were no wagons and few horses waiting on the dusty street.

"What day of the week you reckon it is?" he said.

"How the hell do I know?" Lynch said. "Ain't Saturday, that's for sure."

They pulled up in front of Murdock's store. While they were dismounting, Murdock stepped out on his porch.

He stared at them, without greeting.

Kelso nodded and said, "Town looks deserted."

"Why not? It's a weekday. Never many settlers in on a weekday."

"Had any trouble lately?"

"Not since the last time you were here. Been no Comanches around since then."

"They went into Mexico on a raid."

"Just so they don't come around here again." Murdock stared at the boy. "Say, ain't that the Hanford kid?"

Lynch said, "Yeah."

Murdock looked suddenly worried. "Something happen out at the Hanford place?"

Lynch didn't answer.

The kid said, "They killed my ma and pa."

"The Comanches? Are they back?"

Kelso nodded. "And madder than hornets. The Mexicans down there wiped out half of them." He paused. "They burned out two other places south of the Hanford's that we know of. Killed seven people."

"Jesus Christ!"

"I'll get even," the boy said. "You sell me a gun, mister, and I'll get even."

Murdock dropped his glance to the youngster. "I guess you sure would try," he said. Then to Kelso, "You think they'll head this way?"

"They went east from the Hanford's, way I read their sign."

"What for?"

"Who knows?"

"They could easy swing north."

"They could. But I counted twenty of them left. Them Mexicans down there must have shot hell out of them."

"Twenty, even, is too many for this town this time," Murdock said. "You can see there ain't any settlers in this time of week to help us fight them off."

"Maybe they won't attack here," Kelso

said. But he was finding this harder to believe. "We'll be putting up at the hotel for a day or two."

"You taking Lynch in?"

"Yeah."

Murdock looked at Lynch. "You're in big trouble, Sam."

Lynch shrugged. "I get a Texan jury, I'll be all right."

"Don't count on it. If it was Panhandle Texans you wouldn't stand a chance."

"Won't be Panhandlers — not in Austin."

Murdock looked at Annie, who had her arm over the Hanford kid's shoulders. "What's to be done with the youngster there?"

"I'm going to take care of him," Annie said.

"*You?*"

"You got any better idea?"

"If he was older, I could let him help out around the store."

"Well, he isn't older. He's just a little eight-year-old kid, and he's lost his mother," Annie said. "And I'm going to look after him."

Murdock gave her a strange look. "Well, I'll be damned!" he said.

Annie flushed. "You think I'm not a real woman?"

"I didn't say that."

"Then don't think it, neither."

"Sure," Murdock said. Then, "Emory'll be

glad to have you back at the saloon."

"I may not go back to the saloon."

"Well, I'll be double-damned!" Murdock said.

"You will be, if you don't shut up."

"I didn't mean no offense, Annie." Murdock looked at her torn and filthy Mexican skirt and blouse. "Your credit is good in my store. I got a few plain dresses in stock. And anything else you want to take."

She didn't answer him, as if she hadn't heard what he said. Kelso, listening, knew she was still put out by what Murdock had said.

"I'll get us a couple of rooms at the hotel," he said. "One for you and the boy."

"I got money coming from Emory," she said. "I can pay my own way."

Kelso studied her closely. "Sure," he said. "Any way you want it."

Annie wandered into Murdock's store, leading the boy by the hand.

The storekeeper said, "What happened — where've you been?"

In a few words Kelso told him.

Murdock shook his head. "Don't sound like no pleasure trip. Don't see how you ever made it back alive." Then, "How you fixed for weapons? Looks like your rifle stock is some beat up."

"That's right."

"I got a few guns on hand. Cartridges, of course. Anything you need." He looked at Lynch, then said, "You leaving Sam armed."

"I got his word."

"All right, then. Sam, too. Whatever you need."

"Damned generous of you," Kelso said.

"I got a feeling about them Comanches. If so, we're going to need every gun hand we can get. Still won't be enough. Ain't more than a dozen able-bodied men in town during the week. And like I said once before, most of us couldn't hit the side of a barn from inside it."

"Well, let's see what you got."

Inside the mercantile Kelso picked another Winchester, and he and Lynch both took what they needed in the way of ammunition.

Kelso said, "I get time later, I'll check the way it sights in."

Murdock said, "Do me a favor. Check it out right now and there'll be no charge for none of this."

"I reckon I can't refuse," Kelso said.

He went out and around in back of the store and picked up an armload of cans and bottles from the scatter of debris. He paced off a hundred yards and left a couple of cans, then moved out setting up other targets at intervals up to four hundred yards.

"Ought to cover it," he said when he came back. By the time he'd fired the rounds in the magazine, he was pretty well zeroed in. He memorized the small corrections he had to allow for.

Murdock said, "Damn good shooting."

"Always been right handy with a rifle," Kelso said.

"I feel better already."

"One good rifleman won't help much."

"Maybe so. But all the same I feel better."

"The restaurant open for business?"

"More or less. I got canned goods if you're hungry."

"A full meal would be better," Kelso said. "We been on lean rations. We'll check in at the hotel, then find out. You reckon Rademacher can fix us up a hot tub bath in back of his shop?"

"Hotel will do it."

"Annie?"

She had chosen a simple house dress and some plain underclothes, and a pair of low-heeled shoes, the kind of things a ranch wife would wear. "I'm ready," she said.

They crossed the street to the hotel.

Just before sundown, a drifter came riding in on a lathered horse. He stopped at the saloon and went in. Very shortly, Emory came out and headed up the street to Murdock's.

A few minutes later, they both crossed to the hotel, then from the porch saw Kelso and Lynch and Annie and the Hanford kid leaving the restaurant, and hurried to meet them.

Emory said, "Saddle bum just rode in. He spotted a bunch of Comanch braves twelve, fifteen miles south of here and riding north. He come in a-fogging it, scared witless."

"Piavah?"

Murdock said, "Who else. I had the hunch."

"Round up all the men you can get and let's be ready," Kelso said. "We held them off last time."

"For how long?" Emory said. "Hadn't been for them cavalry, we'd all be dead right now."

"We got to try."

Murdock said, "Yeah, we got to do that. I'll get the boys together." He moved off.

Emory looked at Annie. "Ain't you coming back?"

"I am back."

"I mean to work," the saloon keeper said. "I been expecting you all afternoon."

"I don't know."

"You better make up your mind to it." Emory looked speculatively at the Hanford youngster, then back at Annie. "Well?"

"Seems to me, there's other things to worry about just now."

Emory grunted. "Yeah, you're right." He turned away to follow Murdock, then turned back and said, "Just remember, them plain clothes you're wearing don't make you a ranch girl again."

Annie didn't answer him, and after a moment he turned again and left.

Rademacher passed him, coming up. The barber said, "Well, Lynch, you brought them back on us again. I hope you're satisfied."

Kelso said, "We were behind them on the trail. We didn't lead them here."

"I don't mean it that way," Rademacher said. Then, "When you going to lock this bastard up?"

"I'm taking him in now."

"Too late."

"You trying to tell me my job?"

Rademacher backed off. "My gripe ain't with you, ranger."

"Griping won't help none now."

"It somewhat relieves my feelings."

"Get armed," Kelso said. "Get ready. They might hit us tonight. There's still some moon left."

"All right," the barber said. He scowled again at Lynch, then left.

"I never did like that bastard," Annie said. Then she glanced down at the Hanford boy and her cheeks flushed, as if she was sorry she'd used that language in front of him.

"We'd all better be ready, just in case them Comanches are still moon crazy."

"Don't guess there'll be any cavalry to bail us out this time," Lynch said. "I hope to hell we can hold them off."

Chapter 18

The Comanches were there at dawn the next day. They had come during the night, unseen and unheard by the townsmen standing guard. Kelso and Lynch and a couple of others had taken the earlier watches, expecting that if they struck at night, it would be during those hours. The merchants had taken over the later watches and had noticed nothing.

But at first light, a townsman came to the hotel and awakened Kelso. In answer to the ranger's question, he said, "Look out the window."

The hotel room was at the rear, and Kelso looked out on the prairie and saw them waiting.

"All right," he said. "Get everybody ready. They all know their posts, but try to keep this from the Injuns. No shooting until they make a charge. A first surprise will be the best one we'll ever get. If we can knock enough of them down then, we can maybe hold them to a standoff."

The dawn guard left on a run.

Lynch was up and staring out at the waiting Comanches. "Ever get the feeling you been through this before?"

"Let's go," Kelso said. "They may hit us any minute."

He paused to knock on the door where Annie and the boy were sleeping. She answered at once, and he told her in a few words what was happening and headed then for the street, followed by Lynch.

They took up positions and waited. Here and there at strategic spots, the men of the town were doing likewise.

In a few minutes Annie came out, and she had a rifle, too.

Kelso looked at her and noted it was new, like the one Murdock had given him. "What're you doing with that?" he said.

"I got it last night from Murdock," she said. "Listen, I told you I was raised on a ranch. I can probably outshoot any of these pot-bellied merchants."

"I hope that's so."

"And I'll tell you something else," she said. "If those stinking savages run over us, I ain't going to miss hitting *me* with a bullet. I had my fill of their pawing. I rather be dead."

"What about the boy?" Lynch said. "Would you let him live to be raised a Comanche?"

Before she could answer, firing broke out at the other end of the street.

Kelso swore. "Somebody couldn't wait. Now they know we're expecting them."

"What difference does it make?" Annie said. "Sooner or later —"

"Yeah, I guess you're right. Where'd you leave the kid?"

"In the room. I told him to stay there unless he smells smoke. You think they'll try to fire the town again?"

"Most likely, if they don't overrun us at the first. They come close to burning us out the last time."

She said, "The boy, he wanted to come out and fight, too. Maybe I did wrong, making him stay."

"A little kid like that," Kelso said, "what could he do?"

"Not what he could do," Lynch said. "What he feels."

"What does that mean?"

"You'd have to have it happen to you, before you'd know."

The rising sun glinted on something out in the brush where the Comanches were only partly hidden. At first Kelso thought it was a rifle barrel. Then he said, "Look at that standing buck. Damned if he ain't watching us through a telescope. Could be Piavah."

"Telescope?" Lynch said. "Must have taken it off some Mex officer down there in Chihuahua."

"He's got a 'scope now, besides his bugle. He's getting civilized."

Lynch snorted. "Nothing could ever civilize that bastard." Then, "What the hell would he be looking at?"

"Us, maybe."

Annie said, "If he's picked us out, he'll damn sure hit the town."

"That's a thought," Kelso said. "Get down and stay out of his sight."

Almost immediately Piavah's discordant bugle sounded, and there was a flurry of action in the brush as the braves mounted, and then they came sweeping into range close enough to draw fire from some of the defenders. There was a lot of wasted shooting by the spooked townsmen.

Kelso said, "The damn fools!" He watched as the Comanches turned and rode back out of range. "Now they know what to expect from us."

They waited for a second attack, and it didn't come.

Then a lone Comanche rode out in the open with a dirty calico shirt tied to a stick and held aloft like a flag.

Kelso called out to Murdock, who was the nearest defender who could hear. "Don't shoot. They want to parley. It could be our best bet." Then he added, "Pass the word down the line."

They watched as the brave rode steadily forward. When he got close enough, Kelso could see his curly hair and recognized the half-breed he'd called Chino.

Chino halted fifty yards away. He called out, and Kelso was surprised when he spoke in heavily accented English. "Hello, Texas Ranger. You got the scalp-hunter there with you, eh? And the girl, too."

"What do you want?"

"Piavah, he decides to be friendly. He decides to go back to the reservation. He decides not to kill all of you, if you do one thing."

"What thing?"

"You give him the scalp-hunter," Chino called. "Then he rides away and leaves you alone."

"Go to hell!" Kelso yelled.

"Piavah, he let you keep the girl," Chino called.

In the position next to them, Rademacher was with Murdock. Now Rademacher yelled to Kelso, "Let him have Lynch."

"No!" Annie cried.

"Kelso?" Rademacher yelled. "You hear

me? Most of us agreed last night to do this if we got the chance."

"Not me."

"We knew your feelings. But the rest of us agreed."

"Seems you agreed once before."

"Should have done it that time."

"No way."

"What the hell you mean? You going to buck the whole town on this?"

"If I have to."

Chino, waiting, was listening to all this, but apparently he did not understand all the English. He called now in Spanish, "What are you saying, ranger? Do you and your amigos agree?"

"No!" Kelso yelled.

Chino stared. "No?"

"No!"

"You are a fool then. You will all die."

"Maybe."

"Only the scalp-hunter," Chino called. "You keep the girl."

"No!"

Chino sat there, unmoving, for a long moment. Then he shrugged and turned away and rode back toward the waiting Comanches.

Rademacher yelled over, "You got no right to decide this, Kelso."

"I make it my right," Kelso yelled back.

"Whatever happens is on your head, then!"

He made no answer to that.

Now the Comanches went into their typical riding circle around the town, firing as they went.

"That damn circle they always ride, don't they ever try anything different?" Kelso said.

"Not much," Lynch said. "They don't change. They do most everything the way it's been handed down."

The defending townsmen were shooting again and missing.

"Lord help us," Kelso said, "if they overrun us like they tried the last time. Without some ranchers to side us we won't stand a chance."

The Comanches were riding at long range, and in spite of a lot of gunfire nobody was getting hit on either side.

Then, suddenly, Annie gave a startled cry. "Zack!"

Kelso turned and saw the Hanford kid standing beside her.

The kid said, "You killing any of them, mister?"

"Not yet," Kelso said.

"You give me a gun and I'll kill them," the boy said. "They killed my ma and pa."

"You stay down, boy. Some of them bullets are coming close."

Annie pulled him down beside her and held

him with her arms around him. "You afraid of them?" the boy said. "I'm not afraid."

"You're a brave boy," Annie said. "But there are a lot of them."

The Indians rode closer, and the firing grew thicker.

Rademacher left his post and scurried over to Kelso's side. "My Spanish ain't too good," he said. "I want to know just what went on between you and that half-breed with the truce flag."

Kelso kept his eyes on the Indians, shooting twice before he answered. "Just what you guessed."

"You got no right —" Rademacher said, and stopped.

Kelso turned and saw the blood running down over Rademacher's face from a hole drilled in his forehead.

"Dead," Lynch said, and Kelso thought he sounded relieved.

Annie looked shocked. Then anger took its place, and she let go of the boy and moved forward beside Kelso and began using the rifle she'd got from Murdock.

The Hanford kid watched for a moment; then, unnoticed, he pulled Rademacher's pistol from his waistband and held it up in both hands, pointing it into the distance.

Kelso and Lynch and the girl were all firing

now, and paying no attention to him. The boy stood up and wandered back to the street and walked up it a ways, then cut in between a couple of buildings and came out facing the Comanches again. He started out toward them, still carrying the pistol.

A brave suddenly angled in toward him, racing his pony. The boy waited for him, making no move to run, and when the brave got close and reached for him, the boy raised the gun in both hands and fired and missed.

The recoil knocked the gun out of his hands and drove him staggering backward.

The brave grinned and swooped in and caught the boy up and tossed him over his pony's withers, and went tearing straight through the town and out the other side to rejoin the circling warriors.

Annie heard the boy yell and turned just as the Comanche crossed Main Street. She threw up her rifle but was afraid to shoot with the boy draped in front of the rider. She shouted, "Look!" and then they were gone.

Kelso jerked around in time to glimpse them disappear. "How did it happen?"

Lynch said, "Rademacher's gun is gone."

"The kid must have took it."

Annie gave a half-sob. "That brave little boy. He went out to get his own revenge."

"Just like he said he'd do," Lynch said, then

began to swear. "Now the bastards got that little kid. We got to get him back."

The Comanches rode out of range again.

"Now what're they up to?" Murdock said. He'd just come over to see what had happened to Rademacher.

Kelso gestured toward the Comanche position. Chino was coming out again with his shirt-tail truce flag.

"Now what does he want?" Lynch said irritably.

Kelso was silent. He could almost guess.

When he was near enough, Chino called, "Texas Ranger, you are there?"

"I'm here."

"Good. Piavah, he decides to trade."

"I told you no."

"But now is different," Chino called. "Now you trade the scalp-hunter for the boy."

Chapter 19

Lynch's face was hard. He said nothing.

Kelso called, "Turn the boy loose. Go back to the reservation. If you don't, the Army will hunt you down and you will all die."

"Sure, we go back to the reservation. But only if you give up the scalp-hunter."

"What do you want with him?"

Chino called, "We play games with him. Better him than the boy, no?"

"I can't stand torture," Lynch said.

Chino waited, and when no answer came, he yelled, "You want to see what we do with the boy?"

"Oh, God!" Annie said.

Chino turned and signaled in the direction of a hip-high rock. A brave stood up behind the rock. He was holding the Hanford kid by the bound ankles as a shield.

The half-breed called, "You see the boy? You make trade. You don't make trade, you see Comanche smash boy's head against rock."

Annie began to cry.

Lynch looked over at her, but when he caught her glance his eyes fell.

Murdock said, "A hell of a thing, a hell of a thing." He did not look at Lynch.

Kelso did not look at him either.

Chino called, "Well, Texas Ranger, what you say?"

Kelso called back, "We need time. We got to talk."

Chino was silent. Then he called, "Five minutes only."

"I can't stand their torture," Lynch said.

"They'll kill that boy," Murdock said. "What're we going to do?"

"Sam?" Annie said.

Lynch stood up and said to Kelso, "How good are you with that rifle?"

Kelso said, "I can't risk a shot at that buck. Not when he's holding the kid that way."

"That ain't what I mean," Lynch said. "I'm going out there."

They were all looking at him now. None of them said anything.

Lynch said, "Tell that half-breed they got to send the kid out. You won't miss if the kid ain't in the way."

"Miss what?"

Lynch didn't answer. He said, "The half-breed goes back. They send the kid out walk-

278

ing and I walk to them."

"You going to grab the kid and run?" Murdock said. "It won't work. They'll shoot you and the kid both."

Lynch went on, "I keep walking and the kid keeps walking."

Murdock said, "What the hell does that do?"

"The kid gets close, you grab him."

Kelso said quietly, "And they grab you."

"That's where you come in," Lynch said. "And don't miss."

Murdock said, "Hell, he shoots a couple of Comanches, that won't get you free."

Lynch ignored this and said to Kelso, "You know what I mean? You know what you got to do?"

"I know what you're saying, but —"

"Somebody tell me," Murdock said.

"And don't let me down, ranger," Lynch said. "I can't stand the torture they'd give me. I'd scream and that'd get the dirty rotten bastards' guns off. Don't give them that satisfaction."

"You mean — ?" Murdock said.

"For chrissakes don't miss," Lynch said. "Put your bullet through my head. You try for the heart and I may end up gut-shot."

Kelso said in a strained voice, "It's three hundred yards out there —"

"You sighted that rifle in."

"I don't know —"

"I'm counting on you," Lynch said. "You saved my life last year. You can save my death now. Let me die like a man should, not screaming under torture."

"Jesus Christ!" Murdock said.

Lynch said, "And treat Annie right, you hear?"

Kelso saw the flare of jealousy in Lynch's eyes, and it was something he didn't want to see. God, no! he thought. Not when I got to do this. It makes it too much like I'm doing it for reasons of my own.

Chino called, "No more time. You trade?"

Kelso couldn't say it.

Chino called, "Yes or no?"

Lynch yelled suddenly, "Yes! you half-breed sonofabitch."

Kelso found his voice. He began calling out the terms in Spanish so that he was sure Chino would understand them.

Chino listened him out, then called, "The scalp-hunter, he comes without his guns. I tell Piavah." He turned his horse and rode back toward where the Comanche brave was still holding the Hanford boy above the rock.

Annie kept looking from one of them to another. She seemed not to understand what was going on.

Murdock was silent, stunned by what was about to unfold.

The boy appeared at the side of the big rock and began walking toward them.

Lynch stood up but did not move.

Kelso said, "It's too late to back down. They'll shoot the kid if you don't go out."

Lynch said, angry, "Who's backing down? Just be sure you hit the target." He dropped his gun belt and his rifle and started walking fast across the open expanse between them and the Comanches.

Annie said, "What's he doing?"

"He's saving the kid," Murdock said, tightly. "That's the man you turned your back on, Annie."

Annie said, "Oh, God!"

Lynch slowed his walk so that the boy would reach the halfway point at the same time he did.

They met out there, and the kid stopped and said something. Lynch gave him a shove toward the town and went on walking past. He glanced back once to make sure the kid hadn't stopped again, then turned to plod toward the waiting Comanches.

"I take back anything I said against him," Murdock said. He looked over to where Rademacher lay dead. "I wish Rademacher could see this," he said.

"Sam," Annie said. "Oh, Sam!"

Kelso heard her, and the muscles in his jowls tightened. But he was keeping his eyes on Lynch now. He'd have to be ready when the Comanches reached to grab him.

Lynch looked back over his shoulder to make sure he wasn't getting to the rock before the boy reached where Kelso and Annie and Murdock waited. He slowed once again to keep the distances equal, but then the boy got near to the edge of the town and saw them waiting for him and began to run to them.

He reached them just as a pair of braves jumped from cover to seize Lynch.

Murdock's voice cracked as he said, "Now!"

Kelso had his rifle sighted, and his finger started to squeeze the trigger.

But the boy had seen Annie and ran in front of Kelso toward her, spoiling his aim.

He had a moment of panic, then caught the target again as Annie snatched the boy out of the way. He squeezed off two fast shots and dropped both braves as they grabbed for Lynch.

For a moment, Lynch stood there alone and in the open, and his surprise was obvious. Then, by instinct or reflex, he let himself fall, and for a second Kelso was afraid he'd hit Lynch, too. The fear returned as Lynch lay unmoving beside the dead braves. Then, with relief, he realized that Lynch was playing possum.

It must have driven Piavah mad. He came out of the brush, mounted and charging, his battered bugle slung around his neck, all the frustration of his failed Moon Raid and of losing now the object of his projected torture driving him.

Kelso shifted his rifle and put one quick shot into Piavah's chest, driving him back over his horse's rump.

Two warriors rode up, swept Piavah's body up between them, rode a turn and raced away, and Kelso let them go.

Two more pairs swept up the fallen braves lying next to Lynch, and one rode his horse right over Lynch's body as Annie screamed. Kelso sent bullets flying after him, but missed.

Even as they rushed toward Lynch, they could see the war party riding away in the distance, heading in the direction of the reservation, many miles to the northeast.

"They quit," Murdock said.

"Their war chief is dead," Kelso said. "The last one, let's hope."

Annie was right behind him, still clutching the boy by the hand.

They drew near Lynch, and they heard no sound from him.

Annie said, "He's dead!"

"A horse trampling can do that," Kelso said. He felt bad, but he was watching Annie closely.

She dropped beside Lynch's body and began to cry. His hat had come off, and she reached out and touched his head. "We were never more than friends, Sam," she said. "Oh, God, I hope you can believe that."

Murdock had been watching, too. Now he turned away to stare at Kelso. "There's still the Hanford kid," he said. "What we going to do about him?"

Annie got to her feet and took the kid's hand. She faced Kelso and their eyes met.

"That kid needs a ma and pa," Murdock said.

Annie came close to Kelso and slipped her free arm inside his.

Kelso looked into her eyes and saw the answer there. He said, "Annie and me, we just might arrange that."